I0730818

SOPHIA

MAGICAL QUEST OF ROMANCE AND DESTINY

MICHAEL NENO

WORKBOOK PRESS LLC
187 E Warm Springs Rd,
Suite B285, Las Vegas, NV 89119, USA

Website: https://workbookpress.com/
Hotline: 1-888-818-4856
Email: admin@workbookpress.com

Ordering Information:
Quantity sales. Special discounts are available on quantity purchases by corporations, associations, and others.
For details, contact the publisher at the address above.

Library of Congress Control Number:
ISBN-13:   978-1-955459-91-4 (Paperback Version)
                978-1-955459-92-1 (Digital Version)

REV. DATE: 14/06/2021

SOPHIA:

MAGICAL QUEST OF ROMANCE AND DESTINY

By: Michael Neno

ACKNOWLEDGEMENT

This is a way of acknowledging those who have helped me along the way.

To my loving wife Michelle, I owe you a lot since the beginning until now.

To my family and friends, you've been a big help.

Telling my story has allowed me to reflect on how far I've come to inspire more people to look always at the brighter side of life.

And also the fact that I have been supported by the very best, to whom I can only say a truly heartfelt thank you.

INTRODUCTION

There are people, who for one reason or another, do not believe in the existence of a love so great for one person, they would gladly walk away from their relationship if they thought that in doing so the other person's life would be better. Sometimes Fate, or Destiny, will intervene by taking a hand in things to put the two people back together again, as it did for Sophia and me. Sophia's devotion to me was so great that against all the odds, love brought us together and kept bringing us back together, until our lives became so intertwined we stayed together.

At the bottom of our garden still stands an old oak tree despite the surrounding housing estate that towers above the roof tops, like a king looking over his kingdom, so strong and powerful. I often sit on a wooden bench in the shade beneath the canopy of branches and reminisce over my life and the path that led me through my teenage years to this place.

Today I am sitting and watching my wife and children, Kelly and Marree, as they prepare a picnic under the bright blue sky and think back over the years to my youth and the first time I saw the girl who would one day be my wife. It was not a straightforward romance for us. At the beginning we had the difficulty of a vast distance separating us and long bouts of time away from each other, but fate or destiny, call it what you will, kept bringing us back together again, until we stood side by side and said, "I DO".

Her name is Sophia and is the same age as me. She is nearly six feet tall, slender, with wavy jet black, shoulder length hair and with skin the sort of golden brown that one usually only sees on the beaches of the Mediterranean. But she is not on a Mediterranean beach, she is with me and our two children, in the garden of the home we share deep in the heart of the English countryside.

CHAPTER ONE

I often ask myself how someone like me could have become blessed with the love of such a beautiful woman. I am not rich or famous am not handsome; in fact, I am just an ordinary guy with an ordinary life. No, not even ordinary my mind is healthy and works fine but due to a car accident some years ago I have been confined to a wheelchair. Even now, I have to rely on the wheelchair for large portions of my everyday life. Even so, this wonderful woman has stayed by my side helping me to cope with my disability. If it was not for the love and commitment of Sophia and our now two children during this time, I can honestly say that I would have given up and ended it all a long time ago.

Sophia was born in the country of Italy, growing up in a small town to the south of Naples. Whilst she was still a child her family would come to England for their holidays and it was during one of these holidays that I first became aware of her. The first time I saw her was through the window of her mother's car as it passed me as I was walking to school and, as luck would have it, I would soon be seeing a lot more of her.

Her parents had business of their own to take care of whilst in

England and they were not able to devote as much of their time to their daughter as they would have liked so they turned to a local school for help, my school. With her wavy silky long black hair and a smile to die for she would not looked out of place in any beauty contest or on any fashion parade. About five feet eight inches tall with long slender legs she was so beautiful that every lad in my class were soon besotted by her and wanted to ask her out including myself but luckily for me, none were successful. I remember spending a lot of time during my breaks watching her from a distance, trying to think of a way to meet her, as she sat with a group of other girls who had befriended her on the grass bank, which ran along the outside of the old red brick building that served as both a hall and the school gymnasium. None of my ideas were good enough to put into practice, so it came as a great relief and surprise to me when I found out that Sophia had spotted me already and apparently liked what she saw, although I have no idea why. At first I did not believe them when my mates and several of the other girls told me that Sophia was asking questions about me but she was and very soon I was to be given, quite unintentionally by my teachers, the pleasure of sitting next to her and we soon became good friends.

Being seated next to each other I caught glimpses of Sophia staring at me as I did my work, which was both nice and a little embarrassing but the reason why was soon made clear when we started to become more at ease and comfortably talking to each other. "Do you like me?" came her first question to question after having scribbled things on pieces of paper, whispered to me in a voice filled with all the mystery and excitement of the place in the place where dreams come from. It took next to no time for our teacher to reprimand us for talking during class, so it was back to slipping notes to and fro. One of Sophia's little notes in particular I still carry to this day folded up and tucked inside my wallet. Written on a page torn from her writing pad it told of her feelings for me right from the day when she saw me from her mother's car as it passed by and her wishing I would ask her to be my girlfriend which I did. It did not take too long until everyone at school knew.

I remember clearly the first evening that I spent with Sophia away from the scrutiny of my teachers but we were not to be alone. In order for her parents to meet and get to know me better, they invited me to join them for a meal at a local restaurant. This was largely due to Sophia talking continuously about me to her parents and so I accepted reluctantly, owing to my experience of dining out consisting entirely of occasional take a ways and other fast foods now and again. My worries and anxiety were soon laid to rest by Sophia's father, a very well dressed, short, skinny little man, when he ordered pizza and fries with a clearly Italian accent. It was not until the following day that Sophia explained how her father had deliberately ordered the pizza and fries to help to put me at ease, as he could see that I was nervous which I was. She went on to explain how her parents had liked me and so approved of my acting as her chaperone during her stay in this country. This to me was a great honour, as it was obvious just how special their daughter was to her parents and for them to trust her wellbeing to me, was the best compliment that I could ever have wished for. I just hoped that I could live up to their expectations during the coming weeks. The last few weeks of school were to be the hardest time for me, as at every turn I found Sophia being chatted up by other lads in the school including those who had already left but she let the potential suitor know that they were wasting their time and thankfully rarely needed my intervention as if I was big enough to do much about it.

The start of the last summer holidays at school I would ever receive heralded the beginnings of a love, that even Sophia and I found hard to believe could be. In less than a month of our first meeting, it was becoming quite impossible to ignore the chemistry that was building between us. With every day that passed, the two of us could be found together getting closer and closer, so much so that my parents started saying that they would soon need a crowbar to separate us. The long summer days meant we could laze around on the beach not that far away and the evenings were a time for fun and dancing at one of the many night clubs that we could enter, even though we were still under age for entry to most. The end of the night was always the best part as the music changed from dance to soft romantic music. I felt as though I was in heaven dancing on the clouds, when Sophia was in my arms. I will always remember one night in particular; Sophia and I were smooching along to the Righteous Brothers singing a song called Unchained Melody, when everyone else on the dance floor moved to the sides and a spot light was placed on us. We were so engrossed with each other that when the music stopped playing, we continued dancing amidst the cheering and whistling from the crowd that now watched us. As we danced together that night oblivious to the world around us Sophia said, "I love you. When I go home will you wait for me to finish my schooling so that I can come back to you?" I held her closer to me and we kissed like never before, with a passion that could melt ice. At that moment I truly felt as though I had discovered and understood the meaning of life, which for me was the girl in my arms at that moment.

At home it was impossible to ignore the way that Sophia and I had obviously developed some deep feelings for each other but with Sophia and her family due to return to Italy in just a few weeks, it was decided that letting us carry on as we had been would not do us any harm, but how wrong they were. A couple of weeks was to be all it took for us to set plans in motion, which would enable us to one day be together again for good as we both believed we would. Neither of us could have guessed that along the way there would be circumstances that would test us in ways that could end everything.

Our first priority was to exchange personal details about each other's family such as our addresses, so that we could at least keep in touch with each other whilst we were apart. Next, we let each other know all birthdays and special dates within our own family, the purpose being to show commitment to each other's family despite living so far apart. The intended idea of this was to let each other know that our love was still alive and distance would not come between us or spoil our love in any way. I was not entirely sure that all this would work, that is until a letter arrived the following spring from Sophia, explaining how her parents had agreed on her return to England for her vacations and enquiring if my parents would, or could, agree to let her stay with us. Having a spare room enabled my parents to say yes, but only after several weeks of heavy duty creeping on my part. This news was like my birthday and Christmas rolled into one with the added bonus of it being due to last for three whole months.

I spent the months leading up to Sophia's return making plans and arranging activities which would enable us to spend as much time alone together as was possible. This was something wanted as much by her as by myself. I was now sixteen years old and coming to the end of my schooling. Due to this, my parents insisted that I not let Sophia's stay interfere with my final examinations. This was made doubly difficult. Firstly, by Sophia staying at my home and secondly by the way that during the previous year she had done something which I did not think possible, she had grown even more beautiful.

I do not know if it was the makeup she now so expertly wore, or me getting older and becoming more aware of these things but Sophia's emerald green eyes seemed to shine like jewels, captivating my gaze as soon as she walked into the airport terminal when we met her. At the sight of me she dropped her cases where she stood and ran into my arms where we hugged and kissed each other like a scene from some romantic movie. As we hugged each other my nostrils filled with the fragrant scent that came off her body and coupled with the reaction within my own body, I realised that I was now becoming a young man. My heart was beating madly as our bodies seemed to glue themselves to each other with us only breaking off our embrace when a person in the queue behind Sophia started complaining at the hold-up. Once her passport was stamped and we had collected the remainder of her luggage I led Sophia out to the parking bay where a lift was waiting to take us home. Travelling back home was carried out in relative silence, owing largely to the fact that Sophia and I were joined at the lips, kissing most of the time. When we arrived home my parents welcomed her with open arms as if she was a member of the family bringing happy tears to her eyes. Considering the fact that we had not seen Sophia for a year and even then my parents had only seen her once or twice she was welcomed as if she had always been family. As she had had a long flight it was decided that I would take Sophia's luggage upstairs to what would be her bedroom during her stay which pleased me as it was very close to my own.

The first evening was spent discussing the highlights of the previous year from Italy as well as England, with particular emphasis being paid to the lives of Sophia and myself. As the evening drew to an end and we all started thinking of turning in, my mother turned toward Sophia and made a very profound statement. Before leaving us she said in a soft warm voice, "For the last year I've had my doubts about the effect that you have had on my son but after having spoken with you tonight I can see that the two of you have very deep feelings for each other and will be difficult to keep apart." Once mother had finished speaking she departed, leaving the two of us alone so that we could make our plans for the next day finishing off with a long drawn out kiss, a kiss so warm and sensual that I would not have noticed if the house had fallen down around us. In being apart from each other for a year I realised that my love for this young woman in my arms had grown stronger than I dared to think it could.

The following morning, I awoke to the sound of the radio coming from the kitchen, as mother prepared breakfast and father got himself ready to go to work. I showered and dressed going downstairs with the memories of the night before still lodged firmly in my mind. Everything appeared just like any other morning, in fact so normal that I started questioning whether the night before had indeed happened or was it just a dream. I was just about to speak when the door opened and in walked Sophia, looking like the image of a Roman goddess. I can still remember feeling that I must be the luckiest guy alive to be blessed with the love of such an angel, a feeling that has never left me even with the turmoil of falling in love with another girl and having a child by her. Although Sophia and I sat down together for breakfast neither of us ate very much. I think we were both thinking about the coming day together and all the things we were going to do. Every time I looked across the table in her direction Sophia's emerald green eyes where fixed on me the sight of which made me want to kiss her but amazingly I kept myself under control helped by the fact that we were not alone but in the company of my parents. The plans for the day which Sophia and I had made the night before were suddenly set back by my father as he walked out of the door to go his work, as a partner in a car sales showroom when he wished me luck in my final exam that morning. I had completely forgotten all about it.

While I went to school for my last exam and my final day my mother took Sophia shopping so that they could get to know each other better and talk girl talk. I was sure that I would fail this exam as the only thing on my mind was Sophia. The thought of seeing her later made the time pass by quickly and before long the exam was over as was my schooling and I was on my way home again. As I walked in through the front door I was greeted by the sound of champagne cork bursting free from the neck of its bottle and a chorus of, "For he's a jolly good fellow." sung by my mother accompanied by Sophia. With the afternoon being filled with celebrations, Sophia and I postponed our plans until the following day when we would be able to devote the entire day to them and more especially to each other. In the evening, in order for my parents to spend some time together, I took Sophia out for a walk showing her around the village where I lived. The old 14th century church, the Tudor pub where the adults socialised, even the village children's park with its swings, slide, and roundabout before finally our village post office where I mailed my letters to her.

The following morning after eating a hearty breakfast Sophia and I set off on what was to be the first of many days out together. I could not help but feel somewhat under dressed wearing my customary jeans and denim shirt, whilst Sophia wore the type of outfit one would expect to find on a fashion catwalk. I will always remember how I wanted to show her off and proclaim to the whole world that she was my girl but was conscious of the many eyes that attracted to her wherever she went

Sophia surprised me over lunch by announcing that she had a gift for me but I could not have it until she was one hundred per cent certain that I deserved it. She would not tell me or even hint as to the nature of this gift but she assured me that it would be worth the wait. I was happy to wait for my gift with the secrecy only adding to my anticipation of what was to come. As it turned out nothing else was to be said on the subject until Sophia's last night before returning home to Italy again, leaving me wondering what she was making me wait so long for, or had I in some way made her decide that I did not deserve it.

The next few days were spent introducing Sophia to my friends and neighbours, who without exception welcomed her with open arms. She seemed able to sense the love and pride in her that I held, always looking the picture of perfection and acting elegantly. Whenever someone said that I did not deserve a girl like her even as a joke she would come straight to my defence by listing all of my good points and telling them that one day she intended to marry me and be my wife. I have to admit that the first time I heard her say this I was filled with mixed feelings of caution and pride, but even back then I wished that it could be true. Could this statement of hers, in some way be connected to the mysterious gift that Sophia had told me about?

As the days progressed into weeks I remember feeling a terrible sense of foreboding at the prospect of Sophia returning to Italy and even worse was the possibility of never seeing her again. This was a fear that I could not deny to myself but it was kept safely locked away inside. As it was, we were no longer a couple of school kids and therefore we would now have to go out and join the workforce. However, we still, had a couple of weeks together before we would have to say goodbye and who knew for certain that we would not see each other again?

One thing that Sophia had to do in a hurry was to send her parents the post card that she had promised to send them at the start of her vacation and then forgotten. We spent an entire day going around the local town shops desperately searching for a suitable card for her to send to them. We eventually found one at a small newsagent's tucked away up a narrow side street, which carried a selection of cards for all occasions. As we walked along the street, Sophia likened it to stepping back in time, with the cobbled street, the building fronts and the general atmosphere of the surroundings. I had to admit that I had rarely been along this street before. Sophia soon found a suitable card to send to her parents, so we stopped at a coffee shop and had a drink while she wrote it out. After leaving the coffee shop we found a post office and posted the card to her parents, before returning home.

During the last days of her stay Sophia and I were inseparable going everywhere and doing everything together. I remember telling my mother when asked how I felt about her, that being with her made me feel as though I had died and gone to heaven. At that time, I can honestly say that I had never felt so happy and contented with my life. I could never have guessed that the next few years would test me in the way they did.

All too soon the time came for Sophia to pack her bags, ready to leave me again. This time was harder than the year before with the only comfort coming from my parents, telling Sophia that the door would always be open to her. When the final evening arrived, Sophia and I sat silently, watching the hands on the wall clock above the fireplace counting down toward her departure time and wishing that I could top time so she could stay with me. Although we both had our own fears as to what the future held in store for us we swore that one day we would be together again and not just for a holiday. In order to show each other that we meant this, I gave Sophia the Saint Christopher, which I had been given at my christening by my god parents and she in turn made a promise to give me the gift which she had spoken about some weeks earlier, as she had decided that I had shown her that I deserved it and was the person she wanted to give it to. She still did not tell me outright what this gift was but gave me a clue, which left no doubt in my mind what it was. Sophia explained that this thing was something which all girls have when they are born but give away as they grow older, never to get back again. She went on to say how she had decided that I was the person who she had chosen to receive this most precious of her belongings. Words did not need saying in reply to this, as Sophia could see from my face that I knew and understood what she had spoken of.

In the early hours of the following morning dressed in a pair of tight jeans and white blouse Sophia climbed into my father's car and they quietly pulled away from our home and the village, taking Sophia to the airport so that she could catch her flight home. To my parents this was the end of a teenage love affair but to Sophia and me, it was just a temporary setback to the inevitable outcome. Somehow we would be together again.

With the summer over and Sophia back in Italy, it was now time for me to find employment of some kind. Although I had passed all of my school exams, the grades were not good enough to enable me to go on to further education, or to get a placement on a training course with one of the many large companies. Nevertheless, after several weeks of searching I found a job doing manual work on a building site. Not only was it strange getting up in the mornings to go to work, but it felt extra strange working on a site, which only a year previously, had been wide open fields and home to grazing animals. The wages were low but I still managed to save part of them each week towards somehow seeing Sophia again.

As soon as I received my first pay packet I wrote to Sophia, letting her know that I had taken the first step towards our future. A few weeks later came her reply, informing me of her parent's decision to send her on to further education. Her letter went on to say how her parents considered our relationship as just a teenage crush and had tried to get her fixed up with several of their local lads but each time their attempt had failed on the first date. It went on to explain how her parents did not think that we could be together in the way that we had said we would because of the distance dividing us but she refused to accept this argument. After several more pages the letter finished with a Post Script, saying that she was keeping my gift safe and if I still wanted it, I may soon be able to collect. She also wrote, "If you love and trust me don't write to me here again, I will explain why WHEN I next see you." Reading between the lines, I was able to pick up the message to the effect that I would indeed be seeing her again, but it would take time. Although I could not know what she was planning, I knew that somehow we would be seeing each other again. Even though Sophia's letter suggested that we would meet in the future, her telling me not to write again confused me. The negative part of me said that she was politely telling me that our love affair was over but my heart refused to believe this and told me to have faith and trust her. At first this was relatively easy but as time passed, coupled with not having any contact with Sophia; things became complicated especially when a new arrival appeared on the scene.

After six months of no contact between us, I suspected that maybe she had found somebody new, so when the daughter of one of my work colleges started showing an interest in me, I took her out. Mandy was a pleasant girl, intelligent, considerate, fun to be around, cute and cuddly while being a little shorter than Myself and with her long straight blonde hair and blue eyes I must admit, quite sexy but she was no Sophia, which was lucky for me when I found out that she was also several months under age. This was hard to believe as she looked, dressed and acted more grown up than a lot of adults I knew. I took Mandy out several times as a friend only and always behaved correctly, even when Mandy came on strong to me. This I put down to Mandy's age, that is, until she reached the age of consent and I still could not go as far as she would have liked me to go. There was no hiding from it, I still loved Sophia very much and hoped that she still loved me.

The longer that Sophia and I were apart, coupled with Mandy's continuous efforts at getting intimate with me and my getting to like her more and more, I found myself locked in a constant battle between my conscience and my hormones. I can still recall one particular occasion when walking Mandy home after a trip to the cinema, we stopped at a local, quiet spot for a rest, where my hormones, egged on by her encouragement, found us kissing. The sort of kissing that makes your lips tingle and gives a feeling of butterflies in the stomach. With the kissing and caressing heating up we started to lose control of ourselves. I had already lifted her skirt up around her waist and had my fingers inside the waistband of her panties ready to pull them down, when the image of Sophia flashed into my mind and I suddenly stopped, much to her disappointment. After that night in an attempt to keep control of myself, I carried a photograph of Sophia around in my wallet, so that every time I found my hormones taking over, I would take it out and have a good look, in order to remind myself who it was that I really wanted.

As if things were not hard enough for me already, the whole situation became even worse at the works Christmas Dinner Dance, when after sneaking several drinks, Mandy announced to everyone there that we were getting engaged. Although we knew that she was talking under the influence of alcohol this news was greeted with quite a mixed reaction. Whilst Mandy's parents were pleased with the news, mine were in contrast very sceptical of the whole thing, especially as they knew just how deep my feelings went for Sophia. As for me, I was just as surprised as everyone else to say the least, especially as this was as much news to me as the others. Under different circumstances I would have been happy to go along with Mandy but at that moment in time I felt that it just would not be right. Now I had to explain it to her parents and more importantly, I had to explain it to Mandy. After taking her parents to one side I explained the situation to them. They understood and thanked me for telling them but at the same time, emphasised their regret at it not being true because she had set her heart on me. As for Mandy, I decided to wait until the following day before speaking to her as by this time, she was quite the worse for wear.

The next morning, Saturday, I visited Mandy to confront her about the previous night but found myself in a difficult position, when I discovered she could not remember anything of what she had said or done the night before. This made what I had to say even more difficult than it already was. I explained to her that although she was not my girlfriend in the same context as she would like, I considered her a very good female friend, whom I did have a lot of love and respect for but I was not in love with her, like I was with Sophia. After this I had to know why she had feelings for me in the way she did have. "I know that Sophia was totally in love with you, and she came here from abroad and only wanted you. You must have something very good to offer a girl. And you haven't tried coming on to me like all the others who only want sex with me." Once I was sure that Mandy understood and was alright, I left her and returned home to help mother with the Christmas preparations. Whilst mother and I put the decorations up we talked about the night before, with mother saying how both father and she were very proud of the maturity I had shown, in the way I had dealt with it. I remember feeling that there was nothing for me to be proud of and in a way blamed myself for the way that Mandy had misinterpreted the friendship I had shown her, as love. Now things were better with everything sorted out and put into its right place, or at least that is what I thought but very soon something happened which was to affect the rest of my life.

Late that evening as my family were putting the finishing touches to the decorations, our peace was shattered by the sound of the telephone ringing. Father answered the phone and after a bit of quiet murmuring called me into the next room, where he informed me that Mandy's parents were concerned about her, as there had been no contact with her since my leaving her that morning. This was totally out of character for her hence her parents worry. They were afraid that because of what had happened, she might have run away or something worse. Straight away I put my coat on and set out to look for her. I could not explain why but I just knew that I had to find her and bring her safely home again, almost as if my very future depended on her. At about two o'clock the following morning my search for Mandy came to an end, when I found her huddled up and crying in the doorway of the village church. It seemed that after our talk earlier that morning, she had become so upset that she wanted to run away and be alone. I sat down beside her for nearly an hour as she poured her heart out to me and cried on my shoulder, before escorting her to a telephone kiosk so that we could let her parents know she was safe and sound. When we called there was no reply but their answer phone was turned on, so I left the message that I had found Mandy and apart from being cold and hungry, she was well. I added that because there was nobody at home, I would take her to my place and make sure that she got home safely the following morning.

On getting back to my place I made Mandy something to eat and drink, while my mother prepared the spare room for her. While she drank her hot drink and ate the spaghetti Bolognese I had cooked, we talked more about the night's activities and the reasons for them. During the course of the day Mandy had remembered the party and what had happened. As she said, it was not so much what had happened but more the realisation that her feelings for me were a secret no longer. It was about five o'clock in the morning by the time Mandy finally went to bed, enabling me to turn in myself but this was not yet to be the end of the night.

I remember hearing my father driving away from the house at about six thirty, followed by mother leaving about an hour later. All the excitement of the previous day had tired me so much that I fell into a deep sleep, only to wake up a few hours later to find Mandy had come into my room and was now in my bed cuddled up next to me, in just her bra and panties. She looked so peaceful lying there that I could not bring myself to wake her but the feeling of her warm soft skin pressing against mine was almost more than I could bear. If I was to stay faithful to Sophia, I knew that staying where I was, was not the way to do it, so without disturbing Mandy I slid out of the bed and got dressed.

When mother returned home later that morning she could tell from the expression on my face that something was troubling me. With Mandy still upstairs asleep, I sat down with mother and talked about her, trying to make some sort of sense out of the previous day's events. Unfortunately, mother was not of much help to me over this. It transpired that mother liked Mandy and considered her a more suitable partner for me than Sophia, taking into account the fact that Mandy did not live in another country and therefore would not be going away for a year at a time. She went on to say that Mandy's interest in me was more than just a teenage crush as I had said, besides even if it was, had I forgotten that I myself was still only a teenager, be it almost 17. When I asked why she was saying this, mother replied with, "Remember last year when Sophia stayed here. The look in her eyes and her tears when it was time for her to leave showed just how much she loved you". This was a very profound comment which got me questioning my own feelings. She went on to say, "Now I can see the same things in Mandy and I have seen the way you look at her sometimes." I will never forget what my mother told me that afternoon. Although both of my parents liked Sophia very much, neither of them believed that I would ever see her again but I was hoping to.

By mid-morning I decided that it was time for me to take Mandy home, but first I had to wake her. As I entered the bedroom and saw her lying there asleep in my bed, all I could do was sit on the edge and look at her. She looked so beautiful I found myself accepting the fact that I was falling in love with her. I started to ask myself if I was kidding myself by expecting to see Sophia again. For what felt like ages, I sat there just looking at this girl as she lay so at ease, trying to make some sort of sense out of all the things going through my head. My mind was a turmoil of mixed emotions, the worst of these being the question of, "Can I let myself fall in love with this beautiful young lady?" the same one who obviously loved me. I just did not know how I felt and the harder I tried to figure it out, the harder it got. Being so close to Mandy yet at the same time being so far away from Sophia, was making it harder to find solutions to these questions.

On awakening Mandy, she looked up at me and smiled, letting me see for the first time the love in her eyes that my mother had already seen there. As she remembered where she was and how she had come to be there, I noticed a small tear appear in the corner of her eye. With one of my fingers I wiped her it away, then taking her in my arms said, "Don't cry, I am with you now we'll work it out." I then kissed her on the forehead, bringing a nervous smile to her face. In response to my kiss, Mandy put her arms around my neck, pulled she up to kiss me back but in doing so the bed covers slipped down, showing me her perfectly formed breasts. At that precise moment in time I wanted to take Mandy and make her mine but lord knows how I knew it was lust, not love and I pulled back with the image of her breasts clear in my mind.

Before things could go any further, I told Mandy that it was time for me to take her home, and then left the room so she could sort herself out. When she came downstairs and joined us in the kitchen, it was difficult to hide the obvious nervousness she must have been feeling in the circumstances but I was able to avoid touching on the subject. After having a drink, I escorted her home, where her parents were anxiously awaiting her return, once safely back into the arms of her parents, I spoke briefly to her father asking him not to press her too much for explanations as this was a problem that only the two of us could sort out. Before leaving I told Mandy that I would call on her the next day to make sure that she was alright and did not need anything.

That night I had to make a very difficult decision. A decision that if wrong, could have very serious repercussions on Mandy, Sophia or I, maybe even all three of us. The only thing I was sure of was that the decision was mine and mine alone, so it had to be the correct one. After a night of tossing and turning I came up with what I felt to be the answer to my problem. In order to be fair to both Mandy and Sophia, I decided to give Sophia until Easter to get in touch with me, before going any further with Mandy. Now I had to explain it to Mandy and hope that she could understand, likewise my parents had a right to know of my decision, as it concerned them as well. The only person that I could not speak to about this and probably the most important person, was Sophia. My parents gave their opinion Mandy gave her opinion, Mandy's parents gave their opinion but Sophia still did not know a thing about any of it. With Christmas and the New Year passing away and still no contact from Sophia, I started to find myself thinking less of her and more of Mandy, but the arrival of a card for me on Valentine's Day changed everything.

Not only was it from Sophia, but the postmark was an English one. Was she in England? Inside the card was written, "I still love you and I can't wait to see you again. (Soon)" Reading on, her letter said, "If you still want it, my gift to you is safe and waiting for you to collect." finishing off with, "LOVE ALWAYS SOPHIA." I placed Sophia's card next to my bed, beside the one delivered the day before from Mandy. Seeing these two cards next to each other brought home to me the choice I had to make. I had already come to realise that I loved both Sophia and Mandy, but at the end of the day, I still had to choose the one that I wanted to be with the most.

I knew everything about Mandy, her likes and dislikes her hopes and dreams for the future and, more importantly, I knew exactly how she felt about me and where she placed me in her dreams for the future. As for Sophia, it had been nearly another year since I last saw her. What if she had changed, would I still feel the same way about her and what if she had not changed? More importantly, would she still feel the same way about me, I just did not know? All this uncertainty was playing havoc in my mind, so badly that for the first time ever I went to church to pray for guidance. Obviously there was no heavenly voice advising me on what to do but the peace and tranquillity in the church helped me to think straight and see things more clearly.

I was just about to get up and leave when, out of the corner of my eye I saw the shape of a girl kneeling in the prayer position, down at the front of the church. I could have sworn it was Sophia, but as I turned toward her for a better look, she disappeared. Was this in some way an answer to my prayer?

My experience in the church helped me to decide in what direction my life was destined to go. Sophia was the one I must choose but what about Mandy, how I could tell her and how would she take it. This troubled me immensely as I could still remember the events over Christmas. Not wanting to put her through it all over again, I had to be very tactful in how I told her of my decision. That evening I took Mandy out somewhere quiet so that I could talk to her uninterrupted. Although she seemed to take it well, I stayed with her to make sure she did not do anything foolish.

That evening instead of her parents phoning to say that Mandy had disappeared again, she called at my house asking to see me. After explaining that she fully understood and accepted my choice regarding her, she went on to ask if I would still be there for her, as I had said at Christmas. She also asked if she could still stay over, like so many times in the past, to which my parents gave their permission. After spending the evening with my parents and I just watching the television and talking, Mandy got up and after saying goodnight to us, went up to bed. It was not very long after that the rest of us turned in.

Going to bed that night was no different than any other night but it soon proved to be quite different in many ways. I can still remember hearing father's antique clock chime one o'clock, just before the door slipped opened and in through the darkness of my room, I could just make out the shape of Mandy. It was she who was creeping into my room. To my surprise all I could do was just lay there as she pulled off her nightshirt and slid into bed beside me. Thinking that I was asleep she cuddled up into me kissing my neck and whispering, "I love you so much. I wish just once you would make love to me." I know it was wrong of me but the feeling of Mandy's gentle touch and her soft warm skin pressing tightly against me, was enough for me to give into my natural male instincts. During this night of unbridled passion, Mandy made sure that I knew exactly what I was giving up, by choosing Sophia over her.

When the morning arrived, Mandy left my bed and my room, returning to the spare room where she was supposed to have been during the night. Nothing has ever been said about that night but I am sure that my mother knew what went on.

CHAPTER TWO

On a Friday evening towards the end of March, a knock on our door signalled the time for my waiting for Sophia to end. It was father who answered the door and he quickly called out for me to join him there. Thinking there was something wrong, I jumped up and rushed out to him but as I reached the door I could not see any sign of anyone being there. Before I had the chance to speak father told me to close my eyes and not open them until I was told that I could. I did not have the slightest clue what was going on so I went along with him. My eyes were only closed for a few seconds when a voice that I had not heard for a long time said, "Well, are you going to kiss me or what?" I could not believe my ears, it could not be, but as I opened them, standing there in front of me was Sophia, looking every bit as beautiful as I remembered her to be, no she looked better, much better. I had so many questions inside me but I could not seem to speak. Now I knew why my mother had taken so long that afternoon to prepare the spare room and why. My parents had already known about Sophia coming but had managed to keep it secret from me.

Once the initial shock of seeing her again had subsided, I threw my arms around her and kissed her like never before. Once our lips were apart again we went inside to the lounge and sat down, where the questions began to flood out. How had she got here? How long had she been in England? Why had she told me not to write to her? more importantly how long would she be staying?

Sophia explained how her parents had sent her to university in London, hoping that she would forget me and the promises we had made, as they considered our relationship to be nothing more than just a teenage fling. She went on to explain that she had been in London since the previous summer but could not see me as her parents were scrutinising every single thing she was doing. Her parents did not dislike me but were afraid that their daughter would end up broken hearted, so they wanted to make sure that it did not happen. She went on to explain that she had told me not to write or contact her, in order to mislead her parents from the main reason why she had chosen a university in England, that being to be closer to me. As for how long she would be staying with us, she said was up to me. I looked firstly at my parents then back at her before giving my reply, "How long can you stay? How about as for long as you want me to." One would have to be blind, not to see from Sophia's face that my answer was the one she had hoped for.

With the initial excitement over and the time ticking away we all set off for our beds. As Sophia and I kissed goodnight at her bedroom door she said, "I still love you and I'm still looking after my gift for you. It's yours if you still want it, whenever you want it." I was just about to say that I wanted it then, when my thoughts were transported back to a few weeks earlier when I had made love with Mandy. Suddenly I could not say it, all I could say was, "Patience." and go to my room. That night my dreams were of Sophia and Mandy and the reasons why I loved them both. A year ago everything had been so clear to me but now I was not sure of anything.

The next morning, I awoke to thoughts of Mandy, the realisation that she had no idea of Sophia's arrival and the consequences which it meant. Somehow I had to see her alone but with Sophia around, it would be hard to do. Mother as usual sensed that something was troubling me and choosing the right moment asked what was wrong. As I explained my situation and the restless night it had given me, mother offered to take Sophia shopping so that I could go and see Mandy and talk to her. When Sophia got up, mother informed her of her intention to go shopping together and when Sophia asked if I would be going with them, mother told her that I had to go to work that morning for a few hours. This gave me the opportunity I needed to go and see Mandy, so as soon as mother and Sophia had left I set off to visit her. I had already lied to the woman who I had set my heart on.

As I reached Mandy's home I found her standing at her garden gate with her face clearly that she had been crying and as I got up to her she asked," What's happening to us? I dreamt about you last night and I can't explain it but somehow I knew that you were coming to see me now. Has it got something to do with Sophia arriving yesterday, or was that just another dream?" Mandy saying all this surprised me, especially as there was no way she could have known about Sophia's arrival and the only reply I could give was, " I don't know but it's getting my head screwed up." We took the opportunity to go for a walk so we could talk. As we talked, it became clear to us that we had, in some way, shared the same dream the night before but if that was not strange enough, Mandy asked me a question that left me totally speechless. She wanted to know why I had not mentioned about Sophia being in the village several weeks before. When I asked what she meant by this, her reply was, "I saw her in the church. She was down at the front praying; you were there as well. I followed you in because I wanted to talk to you but when I saw her there I turned and left before you saw me." My experience in the church had not been a premonition or a sign from God after all, I really had seen Sophia that day, or had I. I found myself asking the question, if it had been Sophia in the church then why had she not spoken to me, or let it be known that she was there.

Yet again I was finding my head full of questions. Questions such as, had I made the correct choice in Sophia instead of Mandy, I was no longer sure that I had. I knew Mandy as well as anyone could know another, but as for Sophia, I could no longer be certain. I did know that before I went any further, I had to take a step back and review the whole situation. I asked Mandy not to do or say anything about the things we had just talked about until I had chance to speak to Sophia myself. On hearing the church bell chime one o'clock I had to leave Mandy and head off home, so I gave her a kiss and set off, knowing that Sophia and mother would be back from their shopping trip by the time I reached home.

Before confronting Sophia about all of the things that I had discovered about her during my talk with Mandy, I decided it a good idea to confide in my mother first. Thinking back, I am very glad that I did, as mother knew about Sophia's earlier visit to the village. What I did not know was that Sophia and my parents had been planning her surprise for me since before Christmas, but it very nearly did not happen because when she saw me spending so much time with Mandy, Sophia thought that I had found somebody new. Mother had explained to her that Mandy and I were just good friends and thankfully had said nothing about the events over Christmas, or the night Mandy stayed and what I hoped she did not know about. Knowing the truth put my mind at ease over Sophia, but it still did not explain the dream that both Mandy and I had shared.

Later that evening after we had all finished our supper, Sophia and I departed from the company of my parents and went upstairs to be alone and talk more privately. We talked until father's faithful old clock chimed eleven and signalled time for a late night beverage. Just like so many times during her previous visits, Sophia and I jumped up laughing and joking and raced each other back downstairs to the kitchen to switch the kettle on.

Over a hot mug of cocoa, Sophia told me of a great find she had made whilst shopping that morning, which she just had to buy. In her own mischievous way, she would not go into detail when I asked but instead, said that she would show me later after my parents had gone to bed, if I wanted her to. Sophia's statement immediately sparked a flame of intrigue within me which got me looking forward to the time that my parents would turn in for the night. I did not have long to wait as by eleven forty-five my parents had retired for the night and it was time for me to be surprised. Sophia disappeared into the bathroom carrying a plastic bag, giving me strict instructions to go to my room and wait. After about fifteen minutes my bedroom door opened and in came Sophia wearing the most seductive virginal white lingerie I could have imagined.

Climbing onto my bed Sophia whispered softly, "I have been saving myself for two years now because I had to be certain. Now I am sure that you are the one I want to take me and make me yours. If you do not take me tonight my love, I will take you, either way you will get my gift to you". I could not have agreed anymore with her, as this was something that I had been dreaming of for a couple of years, so taking her hand in mine, I pulled her toward me. As our bodies touched I could easily feel her ample yet firm breasts pressing against my chest through her lingerie and her warm lips were so sensual that we were soon kissing passionately, which led to us very quickly to rolling around in the heat of hot electric passion. Unlike my night with Mandy, this time my parents did know what was going on, partly by the way Sophia's bed was not slept in, but mainly because of the cries of passion emitting from her lips while we made love, woke them. In the morning I was the first to leave my bedroom and go downstairs, where I came face to face with mother.

Other than a "Good Morning" she avoided speaking to me until Sophia came downstairs and joined us, then aiming her words at the both of us turning my face bright red said, "I guess that after last night it is probably safe to assume that we do not need the spare room anymore." I turned and looked at Sophia, she in turn looked at me unsure of what was coming next, before I returned my gaze to mother and said that as long as she and father had no objections we would like to share the same bed. I think it was Sophia who put things into the right context when she said, "I still intend to become your wife, so we might as well get used to sleeping together now." Then with a very naughty look in her eye, whispered to me, "That is if I let you get any sleep, especially after last night."

As both Sophia and Mandy already knew about each other, I decided that it would be best for me to introduce them before they met by accident. I telephoned Mandy and asked her if she would like to meet Sophia and me, so that the two of them could get to know each other. Hesitantly Mandy agreed to my suggestion, asking where and when. A time and place were quickly arranged before I hung up the phone to tell Sophia what I had just done. After breakfast Sophia and I set off for our rendezvous with Mandy in the village park. I was dreading the girls meeting and putting me in a situation where I had to face the two people that I loved more than anything else in the world. Remembering the night with Mandy when our passions took control and the previous night when the same thing had happened with Sophia, I was nervous to say the least. The girls quickly introduced themselves to each other and the three of us found somewhere to sit, so we could talk. As we talked together mostly about Italy and of course the men there my nervousness disappeared when the two girls appeared to be getting on. I must admit though, I did feel somewhat sensitive towards Mandy, when I could plainly see a certain amount of pain in her eyes at loosing me to Sophia. The two girls seemed to be getting on well, when true to form the great British weather soon intervened, turning a bright blue spring sky into one of thick dark clouds and rain, causing us to run for cover. Because Mandy's house was the nearest she led us there, where we were able to dry off and relax with a hot drink.

Getting to Mandy's home I instantly became aware of her Mother's uncertainty over the fact that her daughter had just walked in with the guy she loved and another girl on his arm, a sight which, understandably, must have been unsettling for her. Fortunately for all concerned, Mandy's mother showed great restraint by not saying anything and being friendly to all present.

Once dry, Mandy gave Sophia a guided tour of the house before returning to the lounge, where they continued to talk about music, fashion and me. When the topic of conversation turned to me, I made the excuse that I needed to use the bathroom in order to leave the room, that way I could hide my blushes from the girls. I do not know what was said whilst I was out of the room but when I returned, Sophia asked if my parents would mind Mandy sleeping over the following weekend. I told her that I would ask, then reminded her of the time and the fact that we were going out for a meal with my parents in the evening. After leaving Mandy's home, we went home to prepare for our evening out, making sure that we had enough time to make love again before my parents returned home.

The following morning found me struggling to get up and go to work, partly because it meant that I had to leave Sophia at home but mainly because we had been up for most of the night making love and I was exhausted. At work I found it almost as hard to stay awake as I did finding the energy to do my job but a visit from Mandy at lunchtime helped me to face the afternoon. After thanking me for introducing her to Sophia she asked me just what Sophia had thought about us and whether I had told her what had transpired between us. I informed Mandy that Sophia only thought of us as good friends, to which she expressed concern in case Sophia discovered that, for a short while the two of us had been much, much more, than just friends. She also told me that she believed Sophia suspected that we had been, or were still emotionally involved with each other. When I asked Mandy what she meant by this comment she said, "When we were at my place Sophia told me that after making love with you she knew just why we both loved you as much as we do." After saying that, Mandy seemed to become upset and went very quiet. Seeing this, I tried to get her to open up and tell me what was bothering her, to which she said that at that moment in time she was not sure and could not say but if it were necessary, she would talk to me later about it. Then, looking at her watch, she made an excuse about having a very important appointment and left. I did not see Mandy again that week but Sophia spent quite a considerable amount of time with her, whilst I was at work.

When the weekend arrived and Mandy turned up to stay over, as we had arranged, I could not help but get the feeling from her and Sophia that all was not well. I felt that something was wrong and either they could not, or would not talk to me about it. During the weekend the two girls spent a lot of time whispering quietly to each other and on several occasions, when I entered a room that they were in, I was greeted by silence. This made me even more convinced that there was something wrong with one of them, or maybe both. The only time that things appeared anything like normal was at night when we went to bed but even there, Sophia was not her usual self. I felt as though she was shutting me out to such an extent, that I seriously thought about asking them both to leave but we were still having great sex, although I think that at this time we were only having sex rather than making love. Although I tried to get Mandy to tell me what was obviously bothering her over the course of the weekend, it was not until a week later when she stayed again that a situation arose, where I was to find out what was wrong.

It was in the early hours of Sunday morning when I heard the sound of sobbing coming from Mandy's room as I was heading back to mine, after visiting the bathroom. I could so easily have paid no notice to it and walked on past, but I did not. I knocked on the door then quietly opened it and walked in to find Mandy huddled up in a corner holding a photo of me and sobbing her eyes out. At that time, I still had no idea what was wrong with her, so I knelt down in front of her and taking her in my arms asked why she was sobbing, to which she completely broke down and her sobs turned to tears. When Mandy finally stopped crying, she composed herself and started to tell me what was wrong and why she was so upset. She said, "I've missed my last period and I'm afraid that I'm pregnant. Sophia knows but she doesn't know that you are the only person that I've ever been with. I'm so sorry." She explained that it might be a false alarm and that was why she had not told me before. I never wanted to ask it but I had to know, what would she do if she was pregnant? Mandy then looked up into my eyes and said something that brought tears to my eyes. She said, "I love you so much that when I hear you and Sophia making love like we did, in the next room, I can feel my heart being ripped apart. I know the two of you are very much in love and I wouldn't do anything to come between you. If I'm pregnant, I will go through with the pregnancy and have the baby because if I can't have you, then at least through our child, I will still have a part of you." It all seemed so straightforward to Mandy, but it was not. Before going back to my room and Sophia who was still sleeping peacefully, I picked Mandy up off the floor and carried her back to her bed, making sure that she was comfortable before leaving her.

When I got back to my room I sat on the edge of the bed and looked at Sophia lying there asleep and oblivious to what had just happened. She looked so beautiful lying there that I just could not stop looking at her, but what about Mandy? She may be pregnant with my child, if she was, how could I tell Sophia what had happened? With this new revelation I found myself asking whether Sophia would have said the same thing as Mandy, if their roles had been reversed.

My head was in such a tangled mess that the following morning found me back in the church, where only a few weeks before I had prayed for help in choosing which of these beautiful girls was the right one for me. I did not speak to Sophia about my talk with Mandy the previous night, thinking that I was sparing her any heartache this may bring her and besides, Mandy was still not sure that she was pregnant. I remember thinking how two of the most beautiful girls around were in love with me and I, in turn, was in love with both of them. One had travelled over a thousand miles to be with me and was at present staying in my home, as if she were a member of the family and the other was as equally devoted to me, plus she may be pregnant with my child. All this was happening to me before I was even eighteen years old. Could things possibly get worse, they could and very soon would.

It was a week later that everything came to a head. The Saturday morning saw the arrival of a letter from Mandy addressed to me. In it she explains how the previous day she had visited her doctor and was told that her pregnancy test had proved positive. Due to this she was going away and would not be telling people where she was going to, with only one exception. I read on, thinking and I guess hoping, that I was the one exception mentioned but I was not. The letter did say that in time she would let me know where she was and if I wanted to, she would let me see our child but until then I was not to try and find her. Needless to say I rushed straight around to her home, hoping to catch her before she left and talk her into staying but I was too late. As if all this was not bad enough already, I returned home in time to see Sophia's father loading her bags into the back of his car.

It appeared that Sophia had neglected to inform her parents of her recent whereabouts, thus causing them considerable upset and worry. As a last resort to finding Sophia, her father had travelled to my place in the hope that I might know something that would help him to find her. After everything had been loaded into the car, we gave each other one long last hug before she climbed into the rear of the car, with tears pouring down her face. As the car was pulling away, she stuck her head out of the window and shouted, "I'll find a way to get back to you. Oh and I'll keep you in touch with how Mandy and your baby are getting on." I could not believe it; Mandy had confided in Sophia everything that had happened between us but Sophia had never told me she knew. Now Sophia knew about Mandy and I it struck me that Sophia's father turning up when he did was more than a coincidence. Maybe Sophia had called him to come and pick her up and take her away from here, but if that was the case, why had she called out to me as she was driven away. The next thing that went through my mind was, how could Mandy keep in touch with Sophia with her being taken back to Italy and how would I know if Mandy needed me, or even wanted me. After all, I had rejected her in favour of another. At that moment in time the only thing important to me was to find Mandy, so that I could look after her and my baby when it came.

To suddenly loose both Sophia and Mandy within the space of twenty-four hours of each other weighed very heavily on my mind, turning me into an empty shell of a man and blaming myself for everything. My only conciliation at this time were the words that Sophia had shouted from the car as she was driven away from me in that, she would find a way to get back to me. To me, the thought of seeing her again was the only thing that helped me to keep a grip on reality. Not just that but it appeared Sophia was my only link to Mandy, who I was already missing like crazy and my unborn child. For Sophia not to walk out or even tell me that she knew everything must have been hell for her, especially as Mandy had stayed with us on several consecutive weekends and slept in the next room.

One thing I had to do and I think the hardest thing that I had ever had to do up until then, was to tell my parents what had happened.

Before I could tell them, I had to choose the right moment. On a Wednesday evening about a week later, as we sat down for our evening meal I built up the courage I needed and said. "Mum, Dad, there is something that I need to tell you about Mandy." I paused for a while, before taking a deep breath and continued with what I had to say. "I can only blame myself for her going away like she did." My parents put down their knives and forks and turned their attention towards me. I carried on, "Some weeks back before Sophia returned, Mandy and I went a bit too far when she slept over and now she is pregnant. I didn't know for definite until Sophia was leaving. She told me from the car window as she was driven away from here." Father's mouth dropped open and a look of total surprise, shock and disbelief came across his face on hearing my revelation, but when I looked at my mother I felt as though she knew and was expecting it. When asked what I intended to do about it, all I could say was that I could not do anything until I found her again and then we would work it out, providing that she wanted me. As for Sophia, I could not deny that I loved her deeply but I had to do the right thing by my child and take care of both it and Mandy, the baby's mother, whom I also loved.

Another thing that I had to do was tell Mandy's parents what had happened and to find out if they knew where she was, or how to contact her. Her mother became understandably upset and angry at me over what had happened and I am relieved that she did not have a gun as I have no doubt in my mind that I would now be dead. Having seen the way that all this had affected his wife, Mandy's father swung his clenched fist, hitting me in the mouth and knocking me across the room and on to the floor. With blood coming out of my mouth, I struggled back to my feet just in time to see Jim's face red with anger, looming towards me as he took hold of my collar, dragged me to the door and threw me out of his home.

When I reached home my parents were, to say the least, upset by Mandy's parents' response to my being honest enough to tell them what I knew but understood why they reacted as they did. Believing that I deserved what had just happened to me, I wanted to forget the whole thing but then came a visit from the police, investigating Mandy's disappearance. After telling the officer all that I knew, he made a note of Sophia's address back in Italy and departed. I never knew at the time but my mother had known about the Mandy situation all along and had told the police, hence the reason why I heard nothing more from them.

As the days progressed into weeks and the weeks in turn rolled into months, I slowly began to get my life back into some sort of order. At work there was plenty of overtime available, which I took up, serving me in two ways. Firstly, the busier I kept myself meant that I had less time for crying over Sophia and Mandy and secondly, the more hours I worked meant more money in my pay packet and this in turn meant that I was able to save more for my baby's needs, plus for when Sophia came back to me, which I was convinced she would do. I was very tempted to use my savings in order to go to Italy and visit Sophia but I was not sure that she would be in the same place and besides, what if Mandy tried to get in touch and I was not there for her. I could not believe it, there I was, a 17-year-old totally in love with two girls at the same time and neither of them with me. My life was screwed up to say the least, I had truly messed up.

The most lonesome time for me had to be Christmas and the New Year. I will never forget sitting in the lounge looking at the presents around the base of the tree, the sprig of mistletoe hanging above the door and thinking how it all seemed so pointless without the girls there to share it with. I think that in a way I was very selfish because I still wanted both Sophia and Mandy, even after everything that had happened. Thinking back now I do not think I deserved to have either of them and not having neither was partly my own fault but at the stroke of twelve on New Year's Eve I made two resolutions, number one, to find Mandy and bring her home and number two, to somehow see Sophia again. The New Year was starting with me torn between love for the two most beautiful girls one could hope to meet.

During this most difficult of times I started learning how to drive, in the hope of taking my mind off of the girls but this distraction only lasted for the duration of the lesson. I also dated several other girls but each time found myself being unable to react when the subject of sex came up and as a result, I soon became known as a dead loss amongst the girls that I knew. My life was starting to fall apart around me, until my parents gave me some incentive by offering to buy me a new car when I passed my test, so that when, not if, I saw Sophia again, I would be able to take her somewhere nice. I did pass my driving test in the May on my nineteenth birthday.

My driving test was early in the morning, so I was up and out of the house before the post arrived and it was with great delight that I found a small package awaiting me on my return, especially as it was post marked Italy. I was so excited that I tore open the package straight away to reveal a tape, a letter and two cards, one from Sophia and one from Mandy.

I rushed upstairs to my room, placing the tape into my cassette player and sat down on my bed to listen to it. The tape started with one song, " I Don't Want to Loose You." by Tina Turner, followed with a spoken message from Sophia, saying how much she missed me and asking me not to forget her as she was determined to come back to me. Her tape went on to explain how Mandy had sent her a card, asking if she would forward it onto me as she felt it best for me not to know where she was at that time. The tape also went on to say that Mandy was doing fine and missed both Sophia and myself, finishing off by wishing me good luck with my driving test.

This last statement had me totally confused as neither Sophia, nor Mandy, knew about my learning to drive but Mandy somehow had found out. I could only assume that she was not very far away but where could she be, how could I find her and more importantly, did she want me to find her. Another thing that puzzled me was, if Mandy had disappeared before Sophia's return to Italy, then how could she have known about it, unless the two of them had been in touch with each other during that time.

All these worries were soon put to one side when my parents called me outside so that they could give me their present. Parked outside the house was a car, the present that they had promised I would get if I passed my driving test. I jumped straight into it and drove off quickly getting the feel of the controls. As I drove around the village in my new ford escort I remember thinking that now I had a car, my search for Mandy would become easier because I could cover a larger area. It never entered my mind that I still had no idea of where to look for her, I just knew that I had at least to try and find her. I blamed myself for the way Mandy had gone away so suddenly, without even telling anyone, except for one mysterious person that nobody else knew of. If I had chosen her instead of Sophia she would surely still be with me but if I had, I would have betrayed the love and trust placed in me by Sophia.

Although at this time the Mandy situation was a jumble of unanswerable questions, I could not ignore the Sophia one. Thanks to Mandy for explaining fully what had happened and how it had come about, Sophia still wanted me and was determined to somehow return. After a great deal of heart searching and even more creeping to my parents, I wrote to Sophia inviting her to come and stay with our family during the coming summer. I posted the invite with two hopes inside of me, firstly that her parents would have forgiven her for not telling them of her intentions to come to see me and secondly, I hoped She would want to return after all of the things that had happened between Mandy and myself. Knowing that she was at university and so had no money put aside to talk of, I offered to pay for her airfare if she wanted to come. Two weeks later came her reply, a short note, no longer than a telegram which said, "I received your letter, THANK YOU, no need to buy a plane ticket you need the money more than I, expect a visitor at the airport on the first Friday of July and be prepared for a surprise." My immediate reaction to this note was one of great joy, for Sophia would be back in my arms, in fact according to my diary I had to wait for another five months. How wrong could I have been.

During the following weeks it seemed as though everyone around me was noticing a very positive change in my behaviour. The thought of Sophia returning had got me excited and my mother was worried for me but at the same time she suddenly started shopping a lot and locking away what she had bought, before I had the chance to see what it was. One day I asked her why she was acting so unexcited about Sophia coming back and her reply was one which surprised me. Mother said, "Don't expect too much from what Sophia told you because a lot could have happened since you last saw her." From mother's comment and past experience, I should have guessed that she was not telling me everything but my mind was closed to everything, except Sophia and seeing her again.

On the afternoon of the first Friday in July I finished work, cleaned myself up and drove the fifty-six miles to the airport so that I would be there to meet Sophia from her plane. With my heart pounding in anticipation I was soon given the surprise of my life when instead of Sophia coming through the custom's gate, Mandy walked in carrying a small bundle in her arms, a baby. At sight of me, a huge smile warm enough to melt the coldest of snow came across her face, only to disappear as quickly as it had appeared. She came straight over to me and handed me a letter saying, "Sophia's not coming, but she asked me to come and deliver this to you." Handing me an envelope, Mandy went on to say that Sophia had written a letter for me and it would explain everything. Taking the letter, I did not know what to say or do in response to this new situation.

Holding the letter in my trembling hand I worked my way through the crowed terminal and found a vacant seat, where I could sit and open it. I was totally oblivious to the world around me as I carefully opened the envelope, so that I could take out the letter and read it. I was hoping the letter would clarify the whole situation to me because at that moment in time I honestly had no idea what was going on. As I read the letter it explained the whole situation to me and gave me answers to a lot of questions. It said, "My dearest love. I know this letter must be as difficult for you to read, as it is for me to write but we both have to face up to the situation for what it is and accept it. Even if you realise it, or not, I can see that you love Mandy just as much as you love me and I can easily see why. She is a very beautiful woman and she obviously loves you very much. When I stayed with you last year I sensed the first night that you had become very confused with your emotions but I didn't know the reason why. Although I tried hard to ignore it at first, the whole story became clear to me when Mandy stayed over and I heard the sound of her crying after we had made love in the next room to her.

I must admit that I was very jealous of her and was prepared to fight her for you. That was until she told me everything that had happened and how you had already chosen me over her. When Mandy found out that she was pregnant, she decided to leave for the sake of the both of us, and may God forgive me, I was glad that she did. Looking back on it now, I can see that I was wrong in acting the way that I did, so I am sending Mandy and your child back to you in the hope that you can forgive me. I will always LOVE YOU and I hope that you'll be very happy with Mandy.

P.S. If you forgive me for what happened, I would still like very much to visit you all.

LOVE ALWAYS YOUR SOPHIA

When I had finished reading Sophia's letter, I carefully put it back into its envelope and placed it into the inside pocket of my jacket. Not only had Mandy arrived on the plane which I was expecting Sophia to be on, but she was carrying a baby girl, my daughter. I lifted my head and looked through the bustling crowd for Mandy and saw her standing in the same place as she had been when she handed me the letter. She looked so scared and alone. I guess she was confused at not knowing how I would react to her and the baby, especially as I had been waiting for and expecting Sophia to get off of the plane. The realisation that Sophia loved me enough to send Mandy and my child to me like this brought tears to my eyes and with them running down the cheeks of my face, I walked over to Mandy and asked if I could hold our baby. Mandy passed me our baby and I could not help but instantly fall in love with her. I looked over at Mandy and saw that she had tears in her eyes and with tears also in my eyes, just said, "I think I'd better take you both home now." Taking the baby back from me Mandy said, " I've called her Kelly." With that a whole new stream of tears started to flow down my face. I told Mandy that I had better phone home and let my parents know I was bringing her and their grandchild home with me, to which Mandy quickly replied. "They already know." I looked long and hard into Mandy's face and for the first time since she had walked back into my life, I saw she had kept her looks and even more so, I could see her love for me in her bright blue eyes and I knew I still loved her. Putting my arm around her, I led Mandy out to the car park where my car was and loaded her cases into the boot, so that we could go home.

As I drove us home, Kelly slept peacefully in her mother's arms, while Mandy and I talked of the previous year's happenings. It was 10.30pm when I pulled up outside of my home and we got out of the car. As we entered the front door we were met by Mandy's parents and mine, who greeted us so relieved at their daughter's safe return to them. By this time Kelly had woken and was crying for her bottle so with Mandy's guidance, I took on the role of father and gave Kelly her bottle. While I fed her, the two sets of Grandparents discussed with Mandy where she was going to stay. Without hesitation Mandy said, " If he wants me to and will let me, I want to stay with Mike." I looked up from feeding Kelly and explained that if it was acceptable to the parents, I would deeply like to have Mandy and Kelly with me and if they would let me, I would like the chance to try and be a family. This, I think, was what both sets of parents were hoping I would say and straight away they said, "Yes".

We had barely been back for an hour when the doorbell started to ring and very soon the house began filling up with Mandy's friends having, who on hearing of her return were coming around to see her. Very soon I found myself feeling overpowered by all of these attention, so I slipped outside, got into my car and drove off.

It was nearly daybreak when Mandy appeared by my side and said, "Sophia told me how you used to come here when you wanted to be alone." I had not even noticed where I had driven. I was sitting on the same beach, where so many times in the past Sophia and I had sat to watch the sun go down. The beach was clear and the water was calm with only an occasional ripple on its surface. Sitting down beside me, Mandy said in an almost apologetic way, "I know that I'm not Sophia, but I do love you just as much as she does, and if you'll give me the chance to, I will try and be a good partner to you and a good mother to our child." I put my arm around her and holding her tightly I said, "I know you'll be a good mother to Kelly and I feel that you would be a loving partner for me. I just hope that I can do the right thing by you. I do love you, I think I fell for you a long time ago but I also love Sophia and that's something which I cannot forget about but I will not desert you and Kelly." Mandy moved closer to me, putting her hands around my neck and pulling me close enough to kiss. We lowered ourselves back so that we were lying down and on this deserted beach with the sun rising on the horizon, we made love. Thinking back now, I never did ask Mandy how she had got to the beach that morning.

Over the course of the weekend we sorted Mandy's stuff out so that all of her belongings were with us. I remember feeling very humble, when in unpacking one of her boxes, a folder fell onto the floor, it was full of photographs of me and every Christmas and birthday card that I had ever given to her. There was also a diary in which she had written down all of the things about how she felt about me and all her hopes and dreams for the future. I had not really understood until then just how much she loved me and how much it had upset her when I had chosen Sophia over her. I remember asking myself how I could ever make up for all the hurt that I had caused her and justify her love for me.

After we had finished eating our Sunday lunch, Mandy's mother took on the job of looking after Kelly so that my Mother could show Mandy and I something. Leading the two of us up the stairs Mum opened the door to spare room and directed us through. Inside the room we found piles of babies' things, everything from nappies to a cot. Against one wall were clothes and on the floor under the window were a potty, some feeding bottles and a selection of baby toys. I was so shocked at seeing all of these things that I had to sit down. Once I had composed myself I asked Mum how long she had been collecting these things to which she said, "I knew that one day you'd be needing stuff like this but I hadn't expected it to be so soon. To be honest, I was expecting it to happen with Sophia but never mind, both your Father and I are very proud of you and Mandy." I think it was Mandy who answered for both of us when she said, "We'll make you proud of us." Then she kissed Mum on the cheek who in turn hugged her saying, "I know you will."

Over the following weeks it amazed me how in public no one seemed to remember Sophia but I did. It would be wrong of me to forget how she sacrificed her own happiness for the sake of Mandy and her baby. Nobody forced her to give me up and put Mandy on the very same plane that was supposed to bring her to me. Although I was grateful for having Mandy back, I was as equally upset at loosing Sophia, but fate had not finished with her yet. I think that Mandy was aware of my upset at loosing Sophia although she never let it show. I can still remember to this day, how during those early times my days were busy, so it was relatively easy to keep my mind away from thinking of Sophia but at night it was quite a different story. As I lay in bed with Mandy snuggled up close to me, I thought of how I had been expecting to be beside Sophia and when I made love with Mandy I could not help but think back to the many times that Sophia and I had made sensuous love together in that same bed. Everything seemed to be so final now, instead of Sophia I was with Mandy, I had become a father and with that came responsibility. I had to stop thinking and acting like a teenager and face the fact that I was now a man. The sound of Kelly crying for her feed brought the realisation of my new responsibility home to me. It was four o'clock in the morning but all the same Mandy got up and went to Kelly to see to her needs. On seeing the way that Mandy handled our baby with such love and affection, helped me to realise that here was a woman with whom I would be proud to spend the rest of my life and very soon Sophia became just a very happy memory in my life. When Mandy returned to the bed and gently kissing me, reminded me that Kelly would want her Daddy to feed her next time. Kissing Mandy back I whispered, "If we're going to get married you're going to need your rest, so I'd better get used to feeding the baby and changing her nappies." Before I had the chance to finish what I was saying, Mandy had fallen asleep but even then she had a happy contented smile on her face.

It was over breakfast the following morning; I could see from the expression on her face that Mandy had something to say so I asked her what was on her mind. She turned toward me and with a nervous tone in her voice asked, "Was I dreaming last night, or did you really say what I think you said?" Both Mum and Dad looked over our way as if in anticipation of what may be said but their minds were soon put at ease when out of my pocket I took a diamond engagement ring and taking Mandy's hand in mine said, "It would make me a very happy man if you would do me the honour of becoming my wife." Anyone could see the tears filling her eyes as she said, "If this means that you really want it and you want to marry me then the answer is yes, with all my heart, Yes." For a few minutes the whole room was filled with the sound of happiness as Mum and Dad expressed their pleasure at our decision. " Will you come with me so that I can tell my Mum and Dad the news?" Mandy asked, as she wiped the tears from her face. Before I could answer her question, Father interrupted by suggesting that we invite her parents to join us for a meal that evening, so that we could tell them together. It sounded like a good idea, so without telling them why, we invited Mandy's parents to join us at a local restaurant that evening, to which they accepted. That evening, in front of everyone, I got down on one knee and proposed to Mandy, to which she accepted. This announcement dispelled any idea that I would discard her and Kelly so that I could run off to be with Sophia.

That night as Mandy snuggled into me after we had made love, she told me how she had loved me ever since the first time she had seen me, when meeting her Dad from work one day and how she had a told friend that one day she would marry me. As we lay there, we could never have guessed that this would be the last night we would ever spend together and never again would we make love like we did. I would never again hold her in my arms and look into her deep blue eyes, kiss her soft sensual lips or feel her warm breast against mine and her soft skin under my hand. I was coming towards the end of a critical part of my life and I never knew it. If I had known in advance what was going to happen on that fateful night, I would never have gone out but would have stayed at home instead.

When the morning arrived, I dressed and prepared for work while Mandy saw to Kelly's needs. The day was starting just like any other, the household bustled with activity as Mum, Dad and myself prepared to start another week of work and Mandy fed, bathed and dressed Kelly ready for another day. As I kissed Mandy goodbye on that fateful morning, I can still remember how happy and contented I felt with my life and the direction in which it seemed to be heading. How could I possibly have known about the strange twist of fate that was about to happen. Now it seems that the expression "Cruel to be kind." can be labelled to what happened but why it had to be so cruel, is something that I will never be able to understand.

When I arrived at work the news of our engagement had preceded me and I was greeted with an almost endless stream of congratulations from my workmates. Even my boss sneaked out during the morning and bought a couple of bottles of champagne so that everyone could toast to Mandy and I. Not even the sound of rain bouncing off of the corrugated roof of the site office could dampen our joy. I had not realised until then, just how many friends I had acquired through work. Needless to say, not much work was done that afternoon so my boss finished early and sent us all home.

Before leaving the site I borrowed the office phone and called Mandy to let her know that I was on my way home. On hearing my voice, Mandy appeared to become excited saying, "Please rush home to me sweetheart. I've missed you so much today that all I want to do is hug and kiss you.". Hearing Mandy say this made me wish to be home more than I already did. I left the office and made my way to my car knowing that within fifteen minutes I would be home and the woman that I loved would be in my arms. Driving home, I had to slow down several times, as the autumn mist was starting to creep up along the valleys but I was soon home again.

I was met at the front door by Mandy who put her arms around me and greeted me with a kiss saying, "I love you Mike with all my heart." After a long kiss we went inside where Mandy helped my Mother prepare our evening meal and I showered and changed out of my work cloths and into something better. Once clean and fresh I rejoined Mandy and Mum downstairs, where I sat and held Kelly until our meal was served. As we ate the meal Mandy asked, "Can we drive down to the beach this evening and walk along the prom. I want to show Kelly the beach and the sea. She'll like that and maybe pull in somewhere on the way back and have a hot drink." After we had finished the meal, we cleaned up the table, dressed Kelly in suitable clothing and saying goodbye to my parents, set off for our evening out. I wish we had stayed at home that night.

Driving through the winding lanes out of the village I could plainly see that the mist was coming in thicker, so I slowed my speed down to not much more than a crawl. The nearer we got to the beach, the thicker the mist got until finally, visibility was not much more than fifty yards, so influenced by these conditions I turned to Mandy saying, "By the time we get to the beach it won't be possible to see anything. Shall we turn around and try again at the weekend?" Mandy agreed, so I pulled into a gateway to turn around, with the intention of going straight home, settling Kelly down, then snuggling up with Mandy on the couch and watching a bit of television but fate was about to strike a terrible blow.

CHAPTER THREE

Just as I was pulling away again, some stupid idiot who believed he was could break the laws of the road crossed over without giving way and smashed right into the side of my car causing it to spin across the road through the hedge and down an embankment on the other side of it. For what felt like an eternity, the car rolled down over the embankment, crumpling up with the world around us impacting with the large boulders scattered around denting the cars side panels smashing the windows. Even my Mandy's face was ripped open and smashed in by the impact killing her instantly. The rolling over and over of the car seemed to be endless until finally came to rest upside down in a ditch at the bottom. Kelly was screaming and I knew that I somehow had been thrown clear of the car but Mandy was still trapped inside it along with Kelly. For a short while I just lay there on the cold damp grass in agony, trying to comprehend how I had come to be where I was, then like a bolt of lightning striking me I remembered and immediately thought of Mandy and our baby. I cannot even begin to describe the pain that was going through me at that moment but the thought of Mandy and Kelly still trapped inside the twisted wreckage of what was my car was more important and I knew that I had to help them. I tried getting up so that I could get to them but I could not move my legs, they were in such great pain. I tried dragging myself back over to the car but everything below my waist was dead and wave after wave of searing pain was flowing through my entire body. I could not move. I called out to Mandy but she did not reply, I called out her name then shouted it but still no reply. I could hear Kelly crying out in such a high pitched wail that it vibrated through my ears and that gave me the strength I needed to drag myself over to the car. The bottom of the ditch was filled with soggy mud and water but despite this, I could see and smell petrol dripping out from the bonnet as I managed to pull at the car door but it was stuck. Looking inside to where Mandy was, I could plainly see the extent of her injuries. Her beautiful face was now covered with blood, her right arm had been ripped off above the elbow and her body was torn open, with her insides spilling out into the car's interior. There was so much blood pouring out of Mandy's body that the water in the ditch was turning red.

On seeing this I could have easily given up and died but the sound of Kelly's cries from the back of the car brought me back and I knew that I had to free her from the wreckage that now imprisoned her. I will never be able to explain where the strength came from but I managed to pull open the door and get inside to where Kelly was. Thankfully, inside this tangled mess that only moments before had been my car, she was well strapped in so I undone the straps and lifted her down onto my chest. As I pulled myself and Kelly away from the wreckage I could feel the blood flowing from a gash on my head and running down the side of my face. Once Kelly was free from the wreckage I turned my attention towards Mandy. Then like a firework going off, the car in which Mandy was still trapped burst into flames. The air was filled with the stench of burning flesh and I could feel myself losing my grip on things as the fluorescent tunics of the rescue services began to appear from out of the mist before I slumped down and I guess passed out I heard a man's voice calling out because he had found an injured man and a baby.

The next thing that I remember is waking up in a bed. I knew that I was in hospital by the unmistakable smell that one only gets in them but I could not think of how or why I was there. My eyes were still half closed, so everything was blurred and out of focus but even like that, I could see the shape of somebody standing over my body as if an angel direct from heaven was watching over me. As my eyes became focused I could see that the person standing beside me was neither an angel, nor even my own sweet Mandy, as I would like, but Sophia. My mother on learning about the accident had telephoned her and told what had happened resulting in the deaths of both Mandy and her father before adding the news of my being in a coma with serious damage to my spine, to which her parents paid for a ticket so she could get to us in hours. From the expression on her face I could see that she was overjoyed at seeing me wake up, as I was at seeing her but where were Mandy and Kelly. I needed to know if it had happened as I seemed to be remembering, or was it all just a bad dream? I tried to talk to her but no sound passed my lips. If that was not bad enough, when I tried to move, I could only do so from above the waist and then only slightly.

During the rest of the day, there seemed to be a continuous stream of medical staff coming and going from my bedside, making notes and talking amongst themselves. The only thing that stayed constant during the whole day was Sophia, staying by my side as if she were in some way my guardian angel. Looking at her sitting there beside me, I could sense an almost saintly feeling of being in good hands, with the comforting aura emitting from her smile, to the feeling of total safety received from her very presence in the room. Time and again I tried to speak but each time the only thing to come from my lips was silence. I remember asking myself why this had happened to me.

That evening a nurse entered the room, saying that she was pleased to see me finally awake. As the nurse carried out her duties, she and Sophia chatted quietly almost in whispers to each other, as if they were good friends, and did not want to disturb me. After about ten minutes the nurse Debbie, as Sophia called her, said goodnight and moved towards the door but as she grabbed the door handle she turned toward Sophia and asked, "Has he been told what happened yet?" At that Sophia bowed her head shaking it from side to side saying, "I think someone is going to tell him tomorrow. How do you think he's going to take it Deb?" "I don't know, hon." came the reply. What was someone going to tell me the next morning? I had to know. I spent the next hour trying to get some sort of sound past my lips and eventually at 9.15pm I did. Granted it was just a mumble but Sophia jumped up in surprise. She had not expected it. With thirty minutes of trying, I was able to regain my speech be it broken and slurred but I was finally able to talk to Sophia. I asked her about Mandy and Kelly but all she would say was to wait until the morning and all of my questions would be answered.

The following morning after the nurses had changed the drip that had been feeding me, tided up the bed and given me a wash and shave, Sophia came into the room with her usual smile and twinkle in her eyes. After saying good morning, she took my hand in hers and said, "The doctor will be in to see you soon and I'll have to leave you for a while so that he can fill you in on what has happened and answer your questions. Your parents will be in later to see you and I'll come back with them." Before I had chance to say anything Debbie came in, asking Sophia if she would help her to make up the bed in the next room, to which she agreed. Kissing me on the forehead Sophia said, "I'll see you later." then she left the room with Debbie.

Only a couple of minutes had passed when the door opened again and in walked a doctor accompanied by a priest. Closing the door quietly behind them, the doctor walked over to me and sat on the chair at the edge of my bed looking quite perplexed from the expression on his face I could tell that the doctor was about to give me some bad news but nothing could ever have prepared me for what was to come.

The doctor started by telling me that the accident had left me with a broken bone in my lower spine, damaging the nerves, hence the reason why I could not move below the waist but much, much worse was to follow. He went on to tell me how, with time and a lot of help, I may be able to walk again. Then came the bombshell, the priest had accompanied him because after being in a coma for two months, this was now the time to fill me in on what else had happened in the accident. Standing up, the doctor stepped to one side, allowing the priest to come forward and speak. In a soft voice the priest told me that I had managed to save Kelly from the wreckage but Mandy was pronounced dead at the scene.

The priest stayed and consoled me while I cried and prayed over my loss. It was unsettling to me how what had been my yesterday had, in fact, been two months earlier and the woman who I loved and had been beside me saying "I love you" was now dead, it was not fair. I can still remember asking why I was still alive when Mandy was dead, to which the priest answered. "You are still here because your daughter needs her father and besides, the Lord is not ready for you yet." With that, I asked where Kelly was and who was looking after her, to which he told me that Sophia, who had been at my side for five weeks now, was taking care of Kelly and had also been helping to care for me. With that, the door opened and in she came. Satisfied that I would be all right, the priest gave Sophia instructions to watch over me and call him if she thought I needed to talk, then left.

With the priest gone, I was able to ask Sophia how she had come to know about the accident and why she had come back to England. She explained how my mother had written to her after the accident, telling her how Mandy had been killed and that I was critically ill and in a coma. That answered how she had come to know about the accident but it did not answer why she had dropped everything and rushed to this country to be by my side. When I asked her why, she took a deep breath and with a certain hesitation in her voice said, "Even with everything that's happened, I still love you more than anything but when I found out about Mandy's baby I knew that you couldn't turn your back on your responsibility to it, so I helped Mandy and when the time was right, sent her back. I knew that Mandy loved you just as much as I did and she was willing to keep her child secret for our sakes. Because of that I did what I did." She went on to explain how, with my parents both working, she had been looking after Kelly for me, which she really enjoyed doing. She stayed by my side until late that night just talking with me until, gripping my hand in hers, she finally fell asleep on the chair beside my bed.

The next morning two nurses came into my room so that they could make up the bed and wash and shave me. One of the nurses was Debbie, who commented on how Sophia had hardly left my side during the time since she had arrived and how she had been really happy when I came out of the coma. Debbie asked me if Sophia was my lover, to which I told her how we had been in the past but I had been involved with the young woman who had died in the accident. "Oh, you must mean Mandy. Sophia mentioned her but I thought that she must have been a relation or something, by the way that she obviously loves you." came Debbie's reply, to which I asked her what she meant by that. Before I could get a reply from her, the door opened and Sophia came in carrying Kelly who I instantly recognised. Laying her in my arms Sophia said, "I have brought your daughter in to see you because I know that she wants to see and be held by her Daddy." Looking at Kelly there in my arms, I could see her resemblance to her Mother. She had the same blonde hair and blue eyes as Mandy had and I could also see the similarities in her facial features. It was as if Mandy's spirit still lived within the body of her child. With Kelly still in my arms I looked over at Sophia and asked her why she had travelled so far just to see me like I was, to which she answered, "I know what you're going through, we all are. Besides I'm here to tell you that there is no way on God's earth that I'm going to let you give up on yourself, or us. Mandy wouldn't want you to, Kelly doesn't want you to either, so before you even start thinking of quitting I'm here to let you know that your Parents, your Daughter and I, am not going to let you." I asked Sophia, "Why are you so concerned with what happens to me?" to which she replied, "Because I still love you just as much as before, I always will." I could feel the tears building up inside me, when the door to my room opened and in came the doctor with a nurse, asking Sophia to take Kelly and leave the room for a few minutes.

Once the room was clear the doctor gave me a me quick examination before turning to the nurse and saying, " Everything seems to be all right so you can disconnect the feeding tube now." The nurse briefly left the room returning with a trolley full of sterile dressings and other items and disconnected the tubes, through which I had been fed during my coma, saying that I could try and eat something light later that day.

When Sophia came back into my room I was sitting up in bed, supported by pillows and I was no longer connected up to various monitoring equipment. At the sight of me like this, a smile came over her face, through which even I could see that her feelings for me still ran deep. In her eyes I could see that her love for me was just as strong as it had been all those months before when we were last together, before the accident, before Mandy and before the birth of Kelly, my Kelly, my baby where was she? At that moment I needed to see and hold my baby so badly that nothing else mattered to me. Sophia, who had been holding my baby stepped closer to me and placed her in my arms, at which she smiled. Looking down at my daughter lying in my arms so helpless and vulnerable I knew that I had to get better, if not for myself, then for her.

When lunchtime arrived Deb came into my room pushing a wheelchair, telling me that visiting time would be starting in one and a half-hour time but before then she would take me down the hall to the dining room, so that I could get some dinner. With the helped of a physiotherapist I was transferred from the bed and into the wheelchair so that I could be pushed to the dining room and then turning to Sophia, invited her to join us, which she accepted. Taking Kelly in her arms, Sophia led the way out of my room and into the corridor. The corridor itself smelt clinically clean with a strong smell of disinfectant in the air. I can still remember feeling like some sort of circus act, with nurses' heads appearing in the doorway of nearly every room we passed. I asked Sophia why they were looking at me, to which she said, "Don't you know? You are a hero." I asked what she meant by this and she replied, "You managed to save your child's life after the accident despite your injuries. Everyone just wants to see a real live hero. You can't blame them for that, can you?" Although at the time I said nothing, I remember thinking that if I had been such a bloody hero, I would have saved Mandy as well. On arriving at the dining room, a place was found for me at one of the round plastic tables, where the food was served up. Even before my meal could be given to me I became conscious of everyone else's eyes piercing into me, like needles into a voodoo doll. Being under the close scrutiny of so many staff and other patients, I started feeling very vulnerable and left the larger part of my food uneaten. Once I had eaten some lunch Debbie wheeled me back to my room and helped me to get back onto my bed, ready for any visitors that I may get.

The first visitor I received was a reporter from the local newspaper wanting an interview with me, so that I could tell the readers how I had managed to rescue Kelly from the wreckage of the accident. He emphasised the fact that his employers had offered to pay me for my story but I politely declined his offer out of respect for the one I failed to save, Mandy. The initial questions were followed up with more questions, this time concerning my relationships with Mandy, the teenage mother of my child and Sophia, the foreign student whom I had been involved with prior to and during my involvement with Mandy. This upset me greatly, in fact, so greatly that if I could have got up I would have hit him. Sophia, who had just come back into the room soon put him straight and he apologised to me for his insensitively. The reporter left soon after that and a police officer entered the room, looking very official and holding a note pad in his hand, ready to take notes. Standing by the side of the bed this tall, heavily built police officer proceeded to ask me if I could remember anything about the accident, mainly the other vehicle involved. I was able to describe the events leading up to the accident but was unable to give much information about the other car. When I asked the officer if he could tell me anything about the other driver he said, "All I can tell you is that the driver of the other car was over the legal alcohol limit for driving and was killed in the accident." It was not until sometime later that week, that I discovered that the other car driver was none other than Mandy's own father. This meant that I could finally stop blaming myself for her death. Finding this out knocked me for six. My only consolation in this was the thought that Mandy's father himself had died, quite justly I thought, that a man who through his own stupidity had, in a way, been punished for his actions. After about an hour, the police officer finished with me and left, allowing Sophia to re-enter the room, accompanied by my parents.

It was the first time that they had seen me since coming out of my coma and my Mother's eyes were full of tears of joy at seeing me awake again, while Father was his usual quiet, strong, supportive self. Holding each other's hands, my parents told me that Sophia would be staying at home with them until I was given the all clear to return home and she would also be seeing to Kelly's needs. We talked for what seemed like hours before Dad got up and said that it was time for them to go, so other rose to her feet and said goodbye. As she walked towards the door, she turned her head back and said, "She still loves you Mike." "Who?" I asked, "Sophia! silly." came the reply. I knew that Sophia still loved me as I did her, but I was still in mourning for Mandy. I still had not had the chance to say goodbye to her properly yet and I knew it was something that I must do.

That week I asked permission from the doctor to be taken to the church where Mandy had been buried, to which he agreed on condition that a nurse went with me, in case of any difficulties. Obviously I would not be able to drive myself, so I would have to find a person willing to do so or book a taxi. Someone must have told Sophia that I had asked for permission to leave the hospital and go to Mandy's grave because no sooner had she arrived that evening, then she offered to drive me to the church and visit the grave. Without the slightest hesitation I accepted Sophia's offer, then all I had to do was arrange for a nurse to go along, as the doctor had specified. I did not even have to worry about that because Sophia had already asked Debbie, who had agreed to come with us.

On Sunday morning the following week, Sophia arrived accompanied by a nurse to help me to get ready for the visit to church and Mandy's grave. She brought a bouquet of fresh roses with her, so that I could place them onto the grave because she knew firstly that roses were Mandy's favourite and because she also knew that I would like to place something there. As the time came to leave I could feel something building inside of me that I just cannot describe. It was a mixture of sadness, nervousness and, to a small extent fear. Sadness at the thought that I was going to where my child's mother laid, nervousness over going outside into the open world for the first time since the accident and the fear that I would break down and cry in front of everyone around me.

It was not until we arrived at the church that I truly became aware of my situation, being that now, to everyone else I was just another cripple in a wheelchair, to be pitied, looked over and talked about, rather than talked too. I had ceased to exist as a normal man now and it hurt more than anything. I found myself becoming very self-judgmental, seeing only what I could not do and, what I wasn't. I was losing my self-esteem and ultimately my will to continue living but Sophia's steady hand on my shoulder brought me back and reminded me of the reason why I was there, to visit Mandy's grave.

In a secluded corner of the graveyard, under the shade of a willow tree, I came face to face with Mandy's last resting place. Surrounded by flowers, at the head of which was a marble headstone engraved with Mandy's name and R.I.P. At the base of the headstone was a framed picture of her, to show anyone who saw it just how beautiful she was.

Looking at this soon had tears flowing down my face, as I remembered just how much I loved her. Her smile, her laugh, the perfume she wore, the way she dressed, her soft kiss and the way we made love were all filling my head with such happy memories but more powerful than these was the warmth and love in her face, as she held our daughter in her arms. Then it hit me why I had to stop feeling sorry for myself. Our daughter, Kelly needed a father to protect and look after her while she grew up, but how could a disabled father, be able to do everything. I would need so much help and from where would it come? Although I had not realised it, the answer was closer to me than I knew. Even with all these feelings inside of me I was still aware of Sophia standing there beside me, wanting to look after Kelly and myself. Even crippled up like I was, Sophia was a tower of strength, still treating me as I was before that terrible accident.

I should have realised that there was a greater reason for Sophia being by my side at that particular moment but I was too engrossed in my own thoughts of Mandy and the far too short a time we were together as a family with our baby. Looking down on Mandy's grave seemed to make everything so final, that is, until Sophia placed her hand on my shoulder and said "You need to tell Kelly how her mummy didn't want to leave her and that you are not going to". "I know, help me, I need you?" was the only reply I could give her, to which her reply was the word, "Always". With that, Sophia leaned over me and kissed me so very gently on the lips. After a few more tears we dried our eyes and headed back along the gravel path and out of the graveyard to return to the hospital. Going back to the car on leaving the graveyard, I was hit by something that had never really come to mind in the past but all the same, I too had been guilty of. The way that the general public on seeing a wheelchair, seem to automatically assume that the person sitting in it must be deaf, mentally retarded and unable to communicate, thus they either talk to the person pushing the wheelchair, or look away. This felt very patronising to me but Sophia made me feel less intimidated by it all when she explained that mostly, it was people's misunderstanding and their fear of causing upset by asking questions, which may upset, that made them act the way they did. Unfortunately, there is a small minority of the public, who are just plain prejudice to anyone who is in some way disabled and therefore, in their eyes, not real people and unwanted. Sophia and Deb helped me back into the car and very soon we were back at the hospital, where after having a short sleep I was made ready for visiting time.

After the morning's visit to the graveyard I wanted to see and hold Kelly more than anything and very soon Sophia entered the room carrying her. The first thing I did was to take Kelly in my arms and kiss her, saying how very sorry I was for not being at home for her. In the evening one of the nurses came into see me, informing me that the following morning a person from Social Services would be visiting to discuss my plans for the future and to assess if there was anything that could be done to help. As I very quickly discovered the next morning, the Social Worker was not of any help at all. After a few hours of her talking to me, it was painfully obvious that to her I was no longer a man but just another wheelchair with a cripple in to be talked at rather than talked with, my feelings were completely ignored and I had to put up with being told, that now I was a cripple, I could only do and be what the system said I could do and be. All this hurt but not as bad as being told that because I was crippled my child should be put up for adoption so that she may have a 'proper' father.

During the course of the following night I never slept a wink but cried almost non-stop. My head was filled with doubts as to why I still had Kelly, after a professional had told me that disabled people, such as I, had no right to be a parent or have the same feelings and emotions as normal people. All I could do was to question my ability to be a good father to my daughter and how could I ever expect a woman to judge me and love me as I was now, a man whose legs no longer worked, for most of sociality saw me as a useless crippled up lump of meat in a wheelchair. The doubts in my own abilities became so great over the remainder of the week, that I talked to my parents about going into a place on my own when I left the hospital, rather than go home and spare the family the embarrassment of having a cripple around as at that period in time was mostly the norm, to which my dad said, "So you want to run away from Sophia and your daughter just because you're in a wheelchair now, as a good caring and responsible man would say. Well I think that is the most cowardly thing I've ever heard you say. You've got to face up to your situation as it is and move on, prove to the world that you're just as good as anybody and far better than a lot." He then went on to explain that because of the way I had managed to save Kelly from certain death after the accident, the entire village, my work mates and a very large number of well-wishers had raised enough funds to specially adapt a home for us, finishing off with one last observation being, "Sophia still loves you and I think she wants to be your wife and mother to Kelly. That would make your mother and I very happy as well." I heard what my father said and I knew he was right but at that moment in my life, all I could see were the things that I could no longer do, all because of my disability. How could I ever be a good father to Kelly when I could not even push her pram or pushchair, or play on the beach. I could not go home again until I had come to terms with my own life limitations as it had become. Another thing which weighed heavily on my mind was, although I had never stopped loving Sophia, I had to ask myself how could I possibly be a good husband to her and more so to even think of marrying would be betraying the memory of Mandy.

After everyone had left that evening, I sat alone in my hospital room and thought of where I could go to be alone on my leaving but I just had no idea of where it would be. As luck would have it, the following day an old school friend came to visit me, after hearing about the accident through a friend, who was going to the same university as he was. We talked about our days at school, our lives on leaving and of course our girlfriends. He told me about the girl he had met and fallen for at college and I told him about Mandy and the child we had together. Steve, as he is called, was very upset at the news of the accident and asked if there was anything that he could do for me when I left the hospital. Straight away I told him that I wanted a place to go where I could be alone, to enable me to acclimatise myself to life outside and in a wheelchair. He thought about it for a while then came back with the idea of me staying at his place because of him being away at university it was empty for months on end, to which I immediately accepted. Now I had to tell my parents and harder still, Sophia. I just hoped they would understand that it was something I had to do. As if things were not bad enough already they definitely soon became very complicated, with the arrival on the scene of Kirsty.

By mid-May I had left hospital and moved into Steve's place, a small one-bedroom bungalow with a double parking space outside and very easy access for the wheelchair that I was now confined to. Being in a place on my own I was able to customise myself to life as disabled, while still being able to keep in regular contact with my parents, Sophia and more importantly Kelly.

During June and July, I had started taking myself out shopping, to get into the habit of being responsible for myself and doing everything that an independent person does. It was on one of these trips out that I had my first encounter with Kirsty. As I wheeled myself along the main shopping street a very attractive young girl came rushing out of a shop doorway straight into the side of my wheelchair, falling right over me. I caught her in time to stop her from landing flat on her face and hurting herself, which it appears embarrassed her. Once back on her feet she introduced herself as Kirsty and apologised for falling over me. I noticed tears in her eyes and asked if she had been hurt by the fall. Wiping her eyes, she said, "My boyfriend has just dumped me for another girl and I hate him for it now." and a few angrier things She was obviously very upset so I said, "I know you don't know me but if you want to talk about it to someone, I'm just heading to the Cafe for a drink and you're welcome to join me if you want to." She accepted my offer and we headed off to the café, situated about a hundred yards along from where we were. Once there, I ordered Burgers and Coffees and the two of us sat in a corner where we could be alone while she could tell me her problems. For the obvious reason, I allowed her to carry the tray with the food and drinks to where we were sitting, which she did gladly. Once settled we could talk uninterrupted.

Judging by the speed that she consumed her burger I guessed that she must have been very hungry, which she admitted to being. It transpired that Kirsty's boyfriend had been caught committing a burglary and sent to prison, where he had let it be known that he no-longer wanted her, while at the same time, he would not accept her dating or just being friends with anyone else. At first I doubted this as I could not imagine how a person, locked up in prison, would be able to stop her from seeing other boys but her claim was soon validated when a rough-looking man walked up to her and said, "You know you're not allowed to talk to other guys. Not even cripples like him." I don't know what came over me but I instantly responded by saying, "I may just be a cripple but I can still treat a young lady like a lady, especially a lovely one like Kirsty. So you can go tell your friend that he's just lost out because I am going to date her from now on, and if he wants to try anything bad, he can but say goodbye to his loved ones first coz he'll never see them again. Then turning my head to Kirsty told her it can be if she wanted". I looked at her who in time to see a massive smile appear on her face as she replied with, "Please." With that, the ruffian turned and left the Café, leaving us alone again. Before parting company, I gave Kirsty my phone number, telling her to could call me if she needed to talk at any time. She asked me for my address which I wrote on a scrap of paper, not really expecting to see her again, but that could not have been further from the truth, as very soon I was to find out.

That evening I was surprised by a knock on my door, which on opening revealed Kirsty, again with tears pouring down her face. "What's wrong?" was the first thing I said, to which she straight away replied with, "Everyone's picking on me, I need a friend to talk to. Can I talk to you?" "Of course you can if you want, come inside, I'll make us a drink and you can tell me all about it." I led Kirsty into the lounge where she sat herself down, while I left her and went into the kitchen to make us a mug of coffee before returning to where she was waiting for me. On rejoining her, I positioned my wheelchair beside her and handing her a drink, which I had carried in between my legs, listened as she off-loaded her troubles to me. As she poured her problems out it became quite clear, that on leaving school she had moved into a flat with a friend and because of a certain amount of jealously, was being bullied by other youngsters at the college she attended and things away from there were just as bad.

My unexpected guest and I talked and I listened until almost midnight, when straight out of the blue she turned to me and said, "I can't face going back to the flat tonight can I sleep here? On the couch, or even on the floor.? Please." Seeing her there so upset, I without thinking, said yes. A bad judgement on my part as the following events soon showed. At about two o'clock in the morning I finally turned in leaving her asleep on my couch, or so I thought but I was wrong. I had only been in bed for about half an hour when I was quite surprised by her entering my bedroom, fully clothed and climbing onto bed beside me.

This was something right out of most men's deepest fantasies and yet it was happening to me for real. Once on the bed, she snuggled right up beside and kissed me on my cheek, which straight away started to bring back memories of Mandy and the nights of love and passion that we had shared together, immediately I responded by kissing her back but only gently on her face.

By the time that the morning finally came, thanks to this lovely teenaged young woman just lying beside me, I had confirmation that just because my legs were crippled up it did not mean in any way that I was no longer a man, as large numbers of society believed disabled people like myself to be, but in every other way I was still a man with the same wants, needs and emotions as all others and soon enough the two of us proved it most enjoyably. This revaluation in itself made me feel good but the fact that I had found this out through having sex with a girl that I barely knew, rather than with Sophia, the person that I knew wanted to marry and spend the rest of her life with me, made me feel quite guilty and bad. I looked over at Kirsty once more, still asleep beside me, before getting myself out of bed and into my wheelchair but before I was able to get out she awoke and pulled me back down saying, "After last night

I want you to stay in bed with me for the day and have loads more sex together. Last. night was amazing, I never experienced any of what you did to me before," There was a short pause before she continued with, "I can see all the scars on you. Tell me how you got them and why you're in a wheelchair." she continued, so I lay back and told her all about the accident, Mandy and Sophia. "I can remember hearing about that on the T.V." she continued with, "From what you're saying, it sounds like you're in love with Sophia but you think that if you marry her you're betraying the memory of Mandy. And then in an almost justifying way said, "I reckon Mandy would want you and Sophia to be together." There was a short pause before she finished off with, "but not until you have sex with me again for the day and promise me that I can still be your friend." Inevitably we spent the day in bed having sex, before she had a shower and getting dressed before saying goodbye to each other very satisfied.

That evening I telephoned my mother to tell her of a great decision I had made, although I held back from telling how I had come about it. We talked for a while before she asked if I wanted to speak to Sophia to which I said yes. She called her into the lounge and left, leaving us to talk. Instantly, I knew that Sophia, being glad that I had called, put me at ease because I had been very nervous before picking up the telephone to call her. After some short talk about ourselves and a longer talk about Kelly, I said, "There's something I need to ask you but I need to see you first." to which she immediately said that she would visit me the following morning. Before ringing off I asked her to bring our daughter with her, as what I had to ask concerned her as well. By asking her to bring our daughter with her I suspect gave her a clue as to why which I sensed excitement in her voice.

The following morning, I had barely risen when there was a knock at the door and on opening it, Sophia carrying Kelly, greeted me. I welcomed them with open arms and saw just how much Kelly had grown during the months that I had been away from them, I looked at Sophia and all I wanted to do was stand up and kiss her but it would still be a long time before I could, that is, if I ever would be able to. Even so, there was still something that I had to ask her, but I could not find the words to do it just yet. We went back inside where I made a hot drink for Sophia and poured a class of cold strawberry flavoured milk for Kelly, who had already managed to climb up onto my lap. "Well, tell me, what have you got to tell me that's so important?" asked Sophia, looking straight at me with anticipation. I did not know how to say it, or even if I should, when Kelly asked her a question that said exactly what I wanted to say. She said, "Mummy is daddy coming home with us?" Sophia looked at me uneasily and told me that Kelly had been calling her mummy for about three months, to which I replied that that was what I wanted to talk to her about. Not realising, Sophia started to sob as she tried to explain why Kelly was calling her mummy and apologised, but I soon brought a large smile to her face when I said, "That's what I wanted to talk about." I paused for a few seconds before continuing with, "If you want me, I would be very proud if you would marry me and be my wife making you Kelly's legal mum." Without the slightest hesitation she said, "You need me and I need you! So the answer is definitely yes, on one condition, we get married as quickly as possible and give Kelly a brother or sister." With that, it seemed for the first time, that everything was going to turn out just as we had talked of a long time ago when we were still at school.

Sophia could not wait to tell both hers and my parents the good news, so we both respectively telephoned our parents in order to arrange a get together, which was hastily agreed to. Luckily for us Sophia's parents had come to England two weeks earlier on business and were only about twenty miles away.

Totally unexpectedly, just as we were about to go out to celebrate there was another knock at the door, but instead of me going to answer it, Sophia went. Because I did not go to the door but stayed in the lounge with Kelly, I could not see who was there but the noise of two girls talking told me that it was Kirsty and the sound of one crying was the signal that something was wrong.

When Sophia returned to the lounge, Kirsty, wearing a short

black skirt and quite revealing crop top was there carrying three or four carrier bags full of clothes and visibly very upset. I enquired as to what was wrong and Sophia started to tell me the problem. It transpired that after staying over the previous night, Kirsty's flat mate had kicked her out for getting involved with a disabled guy, as it may affect her social standing if her friends found out. Kirsty had told Sophia exactly what had transpired between us the night before, as I myself had done only a short while earlier, for which she appeared thankful because only that morning I had proposed to her, having fully accepted that my disability did not stop me from being a man, despite what a lot of society believed. Kirsty herself was pleased for us but nonetheless needed a friend and a place to stay, more than anything just then.

We all sat down to talk to try and find a solution to Kirsty's predicament, which soon found us all becoming good friends. As we talked I could not help but notice the way both Sophia and Kirsty where getting closer in the same way as she and Mandy had been. Seeing this pleased me immensely as I myself had developed a strange kind of emotional connection to Kirsty with a love that was not a romantic one or lustful like the very first time that I saw her.

By lunchtime it was decided that, in order to give her time to sort herself out, it would be a good idea if she stayed with me in the spare bedroom and sleep on the bed that doubles as a couch, but only on condition that Sophia and Kelly also stayed with us. I remember feeling that Sophia wanted to stay as well because she feared losing me to someone else, as she had already done to Mandy. She did later admit this to me saying, "I know you like Kirsty but I'm not going to lose you to someone else ever again. The sooner I get a wedding ring on your finger, the happier I'm going to be". I assured her how very much I wanted the same thing as she did, suggesting that we just go and do it as soon as possible.

That night was a very uneasy one for me as I tussled with the idea of firstly getting married, despite my disability and secondly, being able to be the father that society expected one to be but having Sophia laying at my side made it a lot easier. When the morning arrived the whole place was chaotic with Kirsty rushing to get ready for college, Sophia getting both Kelly and herself ready for the day and finally with myself getting ready for my morning visit from a community nurse for the regular check-up. Over breakfast Sophia and I made plans for getting married and letting our parents know what our intentions were. Another thing that I had to deal with was Kirsty and her apparent need for a friend and even more so, help. After a long talk with Sophia about the Kirsty situation, we came to the conclusion that because we both liked and felt for her, she would be welcome to stay with us for as long as she needed. This was something that, when we told her that evening, cheered her up immensely and relieved her because she was greatly concerned about where she would go and this had played very heavily on her mind whilst at college that day.

That night Sophia and I visited my parents and informed them of our intentions, which pleased them greatly. Unknown to her, I had already expressed my thoughts and feelings to mother and a few days earlier with her help, I was able to sneak into town to buy something that was needed to complete the night. After we had eaten a tasty meal I took hold of Sophia's hand, telling her how very much in love with her I was and slid a diamond engagement ring onto her finger, just as I had earlier in the year, with Mandy. We talked for an hour or so about where we wanted to live after the wedding and what my needs would be to cope with my disability, to which my father offered to supply us with the help of some of my old work colleagues. It was decided that once married, Sophia and I would stay at my parents' place whilst we looked for a suitable house of our own and father, with help from others, made the necessary adaptations needed for me.

Once finished, my parents said that they would look after Kelly for the night to enable Sophia and I to spend some quality time alone together. This was very much appreciated by both of us and very quickly we were on our way out to have a drink. This was the first time that I had been to any public establishment since the accident which, to say that I was nervous, was an understatement to say the least and very quickly I was made very aware of the attitudes some people in society.

We had barely entered the premises when a young man who was standing at the bar said, "We don't want cripples here, it lowers the tone of the place. People like you should be put out of your misery." I honestly could not say if it was said in jest or he really meant it but on hearing it my Sophia came out with, "The word disability means not being able to do something." She then addressed everybody present with a question, "Can you breathe under water or flap your arms and fly? NO. That is something that you are not able to do. You've have a disability." Unnoticed by either Sophia or myself, one of my old work colleagues had put his drink down and walked over to us. Now standing at our side, he said with a powerful voice to the youth whose comments had caused such sudden change in atmosphere within the building, "Before you open your mouth again and risk me breaking every bone in your body, ask yourself if you could rip open the door of a burning car with your back already broken, after a serious crash, to save the life of a toddler? " With that the young man's mouth dropped open and silence fell amongst everyone in the pub as they all remembered seeing or hearing all about it on the TV or by reading it in the press. Even the young man whose comment had started all the disturbance couldn't speak higher of me as a local hero which I did not feel like. Although the night's happenings uneased me somewhat, Sophia and I did not have to buy a single drink all night and when we finally left we were quite the worst for wear.

Getting back to my place was the signal for us to rekindle the side of our relationship that had not been there since Mandy and I had been too close to one another. Now, after so long being with me only in her dreams, Sophia could at last be with me in the way that we had both wanted, almost since the first time that we met but in our desire for the night ahead we forgot one thing, Kirsty. We had both forgotten that she was staying at my place and if that was not bad enough, she was sleeping in the next room to us. This was potentially embarrassing as I could well remember the cries of passion that Sophia gave out during our lovemaking. Luckily when we got to my place, it seemed as though Kirsty was either out or had gone back to her old flat, so you can imagine the surprise we got when, after about half an hour of getting intimate on the couch, we entered the bedroom intending on getting into bed to continue and came upon her on my bed curled up and crying.

Feeling as though someone had poured cold water over us, the night of passion that Sophia and myself had hoped for was put on the back burner, so that we could see to Kirsty and give her comfort. Without the slightest anticipation we went to the side of my bed, sat where I parked myself in my wheelchair and Sophia sat on its edge and asked Kirsty what was upsetting her. Even as she asked her question, I could see her eyes enquiring why this girl had chosen my bed to cry on rather than her own and I am sure that I could sense a little jealously. Sophia turned her head towards me and said, "Can you leave us for a while, I think some girl talk is required." Taking the hint, I turned my wheelchair and backed out of the room so as to let the girls have their talk in private.

About a half an hour later Sophia emerged from my bedroom where she had been talking with Kirsty, to inform me that she had confessed to falling in love with me but Sophia had let her know that it was probably just a crush because it was me who had helped her, plus I was now taken by her and after losing me once, she would not stand by and see it happen again. Besides that, she intended on being my wife as soon as possible, so I told her that on the forthcoming Saturday she would be just that. I went on to tell Sophia that I had booked the registry office the day before, to which she threw her arms around my neck and said, "I do I do."

That was enough for us, we went straight into my bedroom, which Kirsty had since vacated and got into bed. where Sophia, who had already been expecting a night of passion, slipped her dress down over her shoulders revealing her beautifully shaped body and bronzed skin. She was wearing some very seductive lingerie, which automatically started my heart beating faster. As she sat on the edge of my bed rolling her black silk stockings down off her slender legs, I could feel myself getting aroused and I wanted to make love more at that moment than ever before. With her stockings off, she unclipped her half cut bra, releasing her firm rounded breasts to my sight. I had already managed to get into bed as Sophia gently pulled back the bedding and slid her body in beside me, kissing my mouth ever so softly at first, then passionately as she snuggled her warm, now naked body right up to me so that I could feel her breasts touching and rubbing against my chest. We lay there touching and kissing for a good hour before Sophia finally positioned herself on top of me saying, "OK I want to feel you inside of me now." and I very quickly felt the moist warmth of her inside as she lowered herself onto my manhood, slowly moving her body up and down. For several hours we made love and as we got more and more carried away with our pleasure, I completely forgot all about Kirsty who had retired into the lounge.

We were still making love when the sound of Kirsty's alarm clock going off and her opening the bathroom door, before knocking on our door asking if we wanted coffee, made us stop. Looking over at my bedside clock I could see it was 8.30am and Sophia and I had just spent an entire night making love. "Please." was Sophia's reply as she turned to me and whispered, "Well aren't you glad you're marrying me now". Putting my arm around her and pulling her closer I answered with, "Did you ever doubt we would end up together my love?" and kissed her again.

Before Sophia could answer there was a single, gentle knock on the door and Kirsty entered carrying a tray holding two mugs of coffee and several slices of toast saying, "I guess you both need to rebuild your energy after last night, I couldn't help but hear what you were doing. I'm so happy for you both." It was not that hard to see a certain amount of envy in Kirsty's face as she said that and hiding the embarrassment on Sophia's face, was equally as hard for her.

Within a few days I found myself positioned at Sophia's side and in front of the registrar making our marriage vows to each other. All this was witnessed by both sets of parents with little Kelly, Kirsty, who Sophia had asked to be bridesmaid and Steve, who had agreed to being my best man. I will always remember the sound of heavy rain thundering against the windows as Sophia and I were making our vows to each other, stopping as the registrar pronounced us man and wife and the clouds breaking to allow the sun to shine through. As we left and stepped outside it felt almost as if the heavens were in some way blessing us, or maybe it was Mandy giving her approval. With the wedding over Sophia only wanted a few more things to make her totally contented, one to become Kelly's legal mum, two to give her a little brother or sister and three to help me to walk again.

Within only a matter of weeks Sophia returned home from the hospital where she had been working part time, to give me the news that she was pregnant and nine months later a son was born who we named Dale, after the American GI who had saved her grandfather's life during the Second World War. All the goals that we had set ourselves had been reached, with the only exception being my still not walking again but even that, with the help of the doctors and physiotherapy was showing signs of coming about. Another thing important to the whole family was Kirsty's continued presence with us. Over the weeks after our wedding, Sophia and Kirsty had become very close friends and Kelly had really taken a liking to her. I myself had learned to rely on Kirsty for certain day-to-day things while Sophia was at work and she herself had come to rely on my help and friendship as well.

Over the next few years everything went smoothly. Sophia and I along with our two children, purchased and moved into a beautiful country cottage in an acre of its own land, a path leading into the garden where I am now sat watching our children at play, while Sophia lays out a lovely picnic lunch for us while Kirsty with her new husband, my good friend Steve, who had been introduced to her at our wedding.

Author's Gallery Over the Years

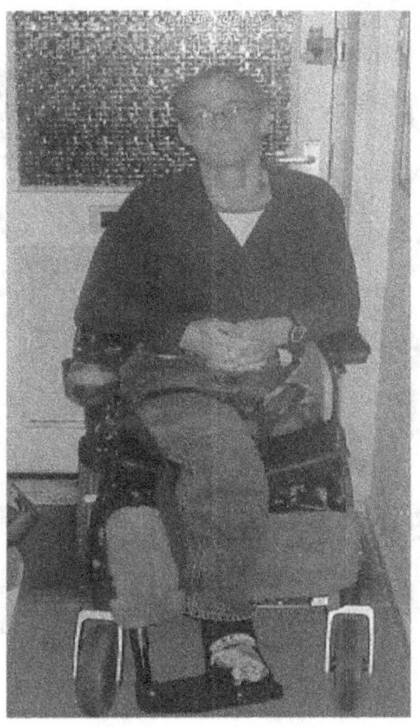

Figure 1. Home after first leg came off

Figure 2. Dressed up for Christmas 2011

Figure 3. Me in 2004

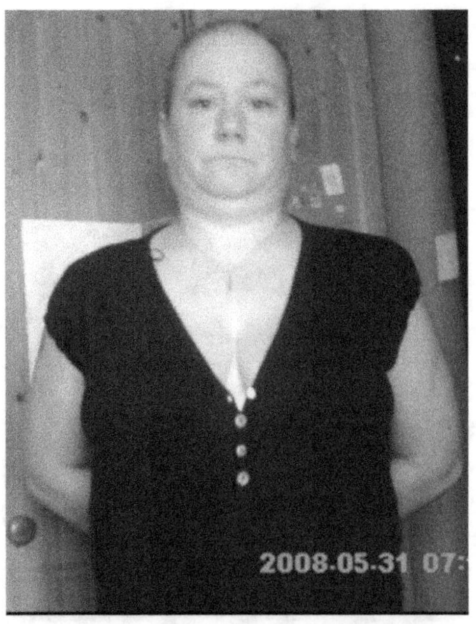

Figure 4. My Lovely Michelle 2007

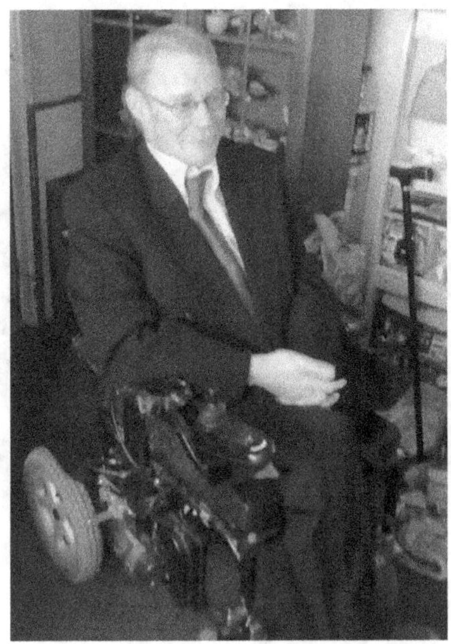

Figure 5. Me with only one leg

Figure 6. My wife Michelle in 2003

Figure 7. Me posing for picture

Figure 8. My custom-built Trike

Figure 9. Wedding day in April 2003

Figure 10. After 3 months using cannabis

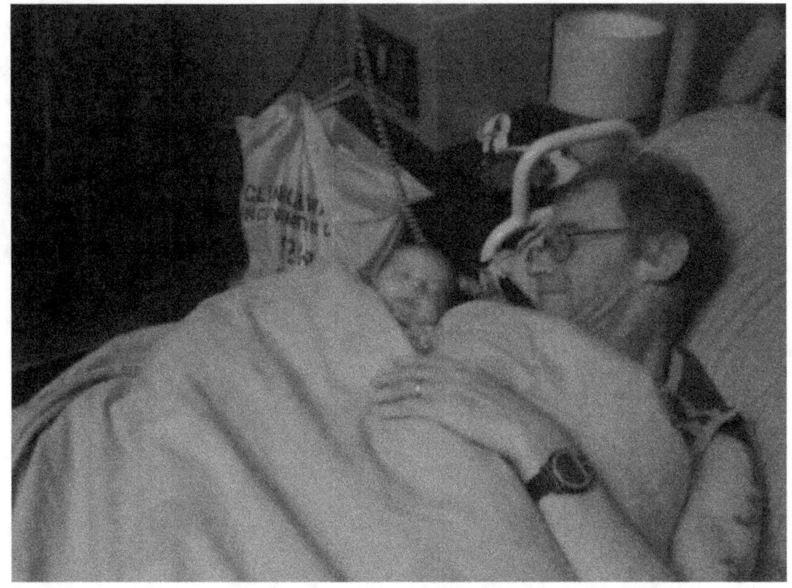

Figure 11. Granddaughter sleeps when grandad is there

Figure 12. Raising money for NABD national association of bikers with disabilities

Figure 13. After 4 months using cannabis

*Figure 14. Me in Year 2012 with my Awesome
T-shirt Sign*